Angela's Seduction

Christopher Fox

ISBN 978-0-9950089-2-2

Published by Christopher Fox, Ottawa, Canada.

Christopher Fox

ACKNOWLEDGEMENTS

I decided to write this novella as a means to introduce people to my erotic novels. Most of the writing for this novella was done personally with no real input from others and I used life's experiences along with research as a basis for my work.

It's interesting that when an author writes about various fictional subjects...killing someone for instance...there does not seem to be any notion that the author has actually done it. However, whenever I tell people that I write erotic fiction, they want to know if it is from personal experience. My response is always that we have all had experience in sex and I just extend my personal experiences with fantasies supported by research.

However, I would like to acknowledge the support of my wife not only for giving me the experiences in sex, but also for reading and providing input to this novella.

Christopher Fox

ONE

My name is Angela and at 42 year's old, I took a look at my life and didn't like what I saw. I had two lovely children with my husband of 20 years, but the spark had long gone out of our marriage. Both Brian and Beth were away at University; one in Calgary and the other in Toronto, so there was just Peter and me alone in a large farmhouse with no other company but the dog, two cats and a coop full of chickens. We had purchased the hobby farm ten years ago after moving out of our first starter home. It was a great venue for us and the children with many areas for shared goals. I was naturally attracted to the lifestyle being brought up on a farm by my parents, as was Peter.

I always considered myself attractive and was able to keep in shape with trips to the gym and healthy eating, but something was missing…no…a lot was missing. I just wasn't satisfied. Peter and I had not had sex for almost two years now, mostly due to his addiction to alcohol and gambling which are likely a result of his diagnosed Post Traumatic Stress Disorder. Peter had done a tour in Afghanistan but refused to talk about his experiences there. Apparently, he spent a few days in captivity before he was rescued by a joint effort of US and Canadian forces. Since leaving the Forces, he took up a position with National Defense as a civilian working at God knows what…it was a high security position and he said he couldn't talk about it, although I knew it was to do with deployment of troops and equipment.

Although I tried to keep track of the money…he agreed to destroy his credit cards and only use what money I gave him…he was borrowing money and getting into debt for which I had to repay. The arguments were getting more severe and he was getting more abusive; so much so that many nights I just went to my room…yes, we were sleeping in separate rooms now…and cried myself to sleep. Peter's nightmares made it impossible for us to sleep together. In the morning, he would be apologetic and win me over again with his charm. It was not that he was a bad person at all…it was his addictions that caused the issues. He agreed to the various counselling agencies and to some extent it would work for a few weeks until he fell off the wagon again. I had shared much of this with my best friend Deborah who was also having issues with her relationship. We met for lunch at least once a week to either compare notes or drown our sorrows. It was at one particular meeting that she brought up the notion of seeking an affair.

"Angela. You just can't keep compromising your life like this. I know you don't want to leave Peter, but there are so many men out there that can provide you with at least the satisfaction you are missing."

"I just can't bring myself to do that Deborah. I take my vows seriously and don't want to cheat on Peter. It just doesn't seem right."

"Look," she said. "I know we share a lot, but there is one thing I haven't told you. I am seeing someone else."

I looked at her with total shock on my face.

"What!" I said.

"I am seeing someone else. It's not that I intend to leave Andy. We just meet a couple of times a month for…well…mutual comfort."

I was still reeling from Deb's admission.

"So," I said. "What does this "mutual comfort" entail?"

"We have mind-blowing sex! Do I have to spell it out for you?"

"Oh! My God!" I exclaimed. "How…how did this happen? I mean, when did this start? Where did you meet him?"

"Hold on," she said. "Let me explain. Andy, as I have told you before, hasn't paid any attention to me for some time. Yes, we have sex now and again, but it is only to satisfy him and not me. There is no desire and very little emotion. It's a wham, bam, thank you ma'am type of scenario. Often when he thinks I am asleep I know he's masturbating next to me, which makes me feel like shit. I felt life slipping away, so

I signed up to this Website that is for cheating spouses…and that's where I met him."

"Is he married too?"

"Yes, he is married with three kids, a dog and a cat. He's in the same situation that I am in and we are very compatible. Neither of us want to change our situation with our current relationships, so for now, it works great."

"Deb, I don't know what to say. I mean, I'm not judging you, but don't you feel shame or guilt?"

"Absolutely I do, but it came to a question of what was best for *me*. I had a choice to make; leave Andy, maintain the status quo or seek an affair. The first two options were not acceptable to me, so I chose the third."

"Where do you do this…mutual comforting?"

"Motels, mostly. We did it in the back of his van one time and once at my place when Andy was out of town."

"Aren't you afraid of getting caught?"

"That's part of the risk and we are very careful…when we did it at my place, he ducked down in the front of the car and we drove into the garage and entered the house from there. No one saw us. We always pick a motel where the cars are not seen from the road. We pay cash, so there is no paper trail. It's just a matter of realizing what you are doing and protecting yourself accordingly."

"It all seems so…clandestine."

"It is," she said.

"I'm not sure I could do that. I think I would have guilt written all over my face."

"You do what you have to do…and you have to do something. Here is the name of the Website I used." She wrote something on her napkin. "Remember it and throw it away…paper trail, you know?"

I reluctantly took the napkin and looked at what she had written. 'CheatingSpouses.com'. Think I can remember that, so I scrunched it up and threw it on my plate.

"Thanks," I said. "I still don't know if I can do this though."

"Just go to the Website and establish a profile. Set up a private email address for all your communications and don't use your name. One of the big Websites was hacked some time ago and all the information was made public. I had a message from some unknown outfit asking for Bitcoins to keep them from posting information on my Facebook page. Luckily, I was smart enough not to use my name or any personal information on the site or the email address I used. Not that someone can post to your Facebook page without your permission anyway."

"I'll think about it."

"Let me know if you decide to do this and we can develop your profile together."

"Thanks…I'll let you know."

We finished lunch and I went back to work. I was a senior administrator in a large law firm and this kept me very busy with many occasions of late night working. It occurred to me that I would have no trouble meeting anyone as I could schedule my work around any clandestine meeting. The thought both excited me and scared me. Was I actually going to consider this?

When I got back to work, I was tempted to check out the Website, but thought better of it. Although I was familiar with computers, I was unsure of how my browsing history could be checked by the IT administrator, so I waited until I got home.

* * * * *

I was able to finish up early and get home at a reasonable time. Peter was not home yet, which was unusual since it was after six p.m.. I had no message that he would be late and started to prepare supper.

Under the circumstances, I decided to make spaghetti and meatballs, because it would not be ruined if he was late. I texted him to ask what time he was expected home and continued preparing supper. When it got to 7:30 and no text or call, I started to worry…he usually advised me if he was going to be late. My stomach was grumbling now so I heaped some spaghetti on a plate, surrounded it with half a dozen meat balls, poured a glass of Chianti and sat down to enjoy it in front of the TV while watching "Jeopardy". At 8:30 I heard a car drive up and a door slam, then watched as he stumbled through the side door totally inebriated. I ran to the front window, looked out and saw his truck parked in the driveway.

"You Idiot!" I said. "You drove your truck in the state you are in? Where the hell have you been?" This seemed to be a rhetorical question, since it was pretty obvious where he had been.

"Fuck off and leave me alone," he slurred.

"Peter, you've got to stop this. At least realize that when you have had too much to drink, get a cab or have someone drive you."

"Don't get on my case," he shouted and stomped off towards his bedroom. "I don't want to talk about it."

"Peter!" I called out after him.

"I don't want to talk about it!" He yelled. "Just leave me alone." With that, he went into his bedroom and slammed the door. I knew enough not to challenge him now.

I went back to my TV program…I was watching a movie but had no idea what was happening now. I pondered on the conversation I had earlier with Deborah and looked towards his bedroom door. I made up my mind that I was going to do it…I was going to put a profile up on the site she mentioned and see what happened. I turned off the TV and went to the study where the computer was. The privacy issue was evident right away since the desk was against the wall and the screen could be seen by anyone walking into the room, and there was no door to the study. If I were to do this, I needed some more privacy. I knew that Peter would be likely passed out by now and would be there until morning.

I turned on the computer, clicked the 'Google Chrome Incognito' link so it would not register in the history log and typed 'CheatingSpouses.com' into the browser bar. Immediately, a page appeared showing a couple embracing. The caption said '…Live again like you've never lived before…' There was a sign-up window and I clicked it. The page then was replaced by a form soliciting information, although no name was asked for. It required a username and password as well as an email address. I was reluctant to provide my personal email address, so I shut it down and decided to go to bed and read.

I started to fantasize about having sex again…about having someone want me and cherish me…make me feel like a woman once more. As I thought about it I put my book down and started to fondle myself. I started by gently rubbing my stomach, then lifted my nightshirt and rubbed my hands on my legs. I liked the feel of my hands on my body and, in my mind, I imagined they were someone else's. I lifted my nightshirt up to my neck and continued to slowly caress myself…my abdomen, lower stomach and then my breasts. I loved the feel of my breasts. At a 38D, I was fortunate that even at my age, they were still firm and I had large areola that were now plump and my nipples firm. I gently squeezed each breast and tweaked the nipples…it felt so good. I was aroused now and could feel it between my legs. I moved one hand down to my pussy and felt the wetness while I continued with massaging my breasts. My clitoris was swollen and it felt heavenly to my touch. Oh! How I wished it was some handsome stud manipulating me. I played with my abundant labia as I moved my fingers up and down from my vagina to my clitoris and back to my vagina. I then inserted two fingers and sought out my G-Spot, tweaking my fingers as I did so. My breathing now became shallow as I pushed my fingers in as far as I could, then withdrew them almost all the way out, then thrust them back in again. I could feel a pending climax as I quickened my movements. I was on the verge of coming when I pulled out my fingers and manipulated my clitoris again. The feelings of pleasure were building within me as the climax neared. I stifled my cries for fear of being heard, so what emanated from me was barely a whimper. I slowed my movements to prolong my finish as the wave of ecstasy welled up and I exploded in a wonderful orgasm, grunting with each pulse despite my attempts to curtail the sounds I was making. My whole body convulsed and shook with each successive rhythmic expansion and contraction. I lay there, naked with the exception of my nightie around my neck, totally exhausted. I fondled my breasts again and tweaked my now soft nipples. I longed for a man's touch on my body, the feeling of his hardness inside me, experiencing that sensation of his juices flowing into me. As I fantasized about what it would be like, I fell into a deep and wonderful sleep.

I awoke the next morning and made coffee…Peter hadn't emerged from his room yet. I wasn't in the mood to make breakfast and decided to grab something at the cafeteria at work. I really didn't want to have a confrontation with Peter now anyway…I was still pissed at him. I thought more about the idea of registering with the Site and texted Deborah saying 'Lunch?' I wanted to go over some details with her seeing as it appeared that she had some experience in this. Just as I was walking out the front door, I heard Peter's door open, but I didn't even look at him. I got into my car and drove away. As I looked in my rear-view mirror, I could see Peter standing in the open doorway in his underwear. My phone dinged and I checked the message…Deborah was OK for lunch. Then my phone rang and I checked the display…it was Peter. I hit 'cancel'.

"Hey Angie," Deborah said as she approached the table.

"Deborah," I said as I stood and we embraced. Somehow, Deborah did not want to go by the shortened 'Debby' or 'Deb', so I continued to respect her wishes and referred to her as Deborah, even though when mentioning her name with anyone else, I generally used one of the truncated forms.

"Peter came home drunk again last night," I started. "What was worse, he drove his truck home."

"Oh, no!" she said, placing her hand over her mouth. "I am so sorry."

"I didn't even speak to him this morning before I left and when he called me I just didn't answer."

"I am so sorry Angie, I wish there was something I could do."

"I've decided to try that site you mentioned, but I need some tips on security. I just don't want anyone finding out. First thing I noticed was that the computer at home has the screen facing outwards and there is no door to the study. Also, I'm reluctant to use the computer at work because I'm sure it is not secure and the network administrator may be able to track my browsing history. I don't trust him anyway."

"OK Angie, let's go over some of the security issues. You're right in that you should not access the site from work...among other things it could be construed as a mis-use of company equipment, plus, as you said, there is no privacy there. What I did was get an iPad. You can connect to your network at home and surf all you want in the privacy of your own room." She reached into her purse and retrieved her iPad and turned it on. "First thing is to put a password on both your iPad and iPhone," she said as she keyed in a number. "When you go to the Safari page, press the little 'page' button here," she pressed the icon and the page receded. "Then press the 'Private' icon here; you'll see the 'Private' button highlighted. Click the 'Done' button and you are now in private browsing mode. This way, none of your history is stored."

"Wow!" I said. "How do you know all this?"

"You forget," she said. "I look after all the IT for the clinic." Deborah worked for one of the local medical clinics and was their 'Girl Friday'.

"When you sign up," she continued, "you can have any new messages forwarded to your phone, but I don't advise you to do that."

"Why is that?" I said.

"Because you will get tons of messages and your phone will be going off all day. This could be embarrassing at work and especially at home."

"How do you know I will get a lot of messages?"

"Trust me, you will get a ton of messages. I think I had almost sixty messages my first day. I think most men message everyone who is new to the Site. Plus you'll get a lot of Winks, but I ignore them. If a guy doesn't know enough to send me a message, then I don't respond. Also, you will get a lot of men who think that they can encourage women by trolling with pictures of their dick. I just delete those right away. There is a lot of garbage, but you just have to sift through it and don't get discouraged."

"OK, I think I can handle that. At least I'm willing to give it a try."

"Good, so let's set up a profile for you. First of all, we are going to set up an email address for your clandestine activities. What handle do you want to use?"

"I have no idea. What would you suggest?"

Let's pick a name that we can use on both your email and the Website. How about 'Hotcountrywife?'

I laughed. "Really?"

"Sounds good to me. Let's see if it's available. Do you have a preference for which email carrier you want to use?"

"Not really. Can we use the same one as I use for my personal email?"

"Sure. That won't be a problem". She logged onto the carrier and keyed in 'Hotcountrywife'. "Great! It is available." She finished setting up the email address and then logged on to cheatingspouses.com.

"OK," she said. "Now let's see if the name is available here." She tried it and said, "voila! Now we just fill in the rest of the info and we're set."

"Here," she said as she turned her iPad to me. "Check it out and see if you think it's OK."

I read it over and said, "It looks good to me."

"OK, it's done then. It's better to put a little more information about what you are looking for, although I think most men just send a message to everyone. Sort of a 'hoist up the flag and see who salutes' type of thing." She pressed the 'complete profile' key and closed the iPad. "Now we wait for the responses. Don't be surprised at the number of messages you'll have by the time you get home."

"I guess I have to buy an iPad now. I'm sure Peter will ask what I want it for."

"Tell him you bought it as a reader. Once you start to read books electronically, you'll never go back to paper books."

"I'm kind of used to the idea of holding a book. I'm not sure I would enjoy reading electronically."

"Everyone says that, but it's the natural resistance to change, especially if it's something you enjoy doing. For years, people couldn't get used to travelling without staring at a horse's ass. With an electronic reader, you can set the text size to whatever you want, so you don't have to squint like you do with some books. Also, you have an onboard dictionary. But the best feature for me is the 'Search' function, whereby you can highlight, say, a character you don't recall. A window will be displayed that shows a few words of everywhere the name appears in the book. I also like the idea that I can search the Web from anywhere in the book to check facts or locations."

"Sounds interesting," I said. "Maybe this country girl will progress to the new age."

I thanked her and insisted I pay for lunch. I then returned to work and made a mental note to buy an iPad on the way home. I must admit that I was excited at the possibilities of maybe meeting someone, but was scared also. The whole notion of going outside my marriage for sex was alien to me…to break my vows. But I had to do something. I just wasn't happy and, like Deborah, I had the three options and options one and two were not acceptable to me.

TWO

I dropped into Best Buy on my home and picked up the latest version of iPad. I was anxious to get home and see how many messages I had from the site. I told Peter that I had bought an iPad to access my work from home so that I would not have to stay so late. I was expecting him to ask why I just couldn't use the computer in the study, but he just grunted and that was that. I prepared supper and couldn't wait to get it over with and check my messages.

"Just going to my room to set up my iPad," I said to Peter.

"OK," he said, not looking away from the TV. It seemed like the actions this morning were forgotten and that was fine with me...I didn't want to get into a big discussion about it. I had resigned myself now to just go with the flow and see if my alternate life made things better for me. I know now I wasn't going to change Peter and one day it may come to us separating, but I didn't want to handle that now.

I unpacked the iPad and turned it on. Fortunately, there was enough charge in it to use it right away. I logged into our home Wi-Fi and used the Safari button to log onto the Web. I logged onto Cheatingspouses.com and signed into my account.

"Holy shit!" I said to myself. There were 53 messages! Deborah wasn't exaggerating about the responses I would get. I opened my mailbox and started to sift through the messages. Many were winks and, based on Debbie's advice, I didn't bother with them right now and concentrated on reading just the messages. She was right also that many of the messages were accompanied by dick pics, which I immediately deleted. I ended up with four that seemed promising. They were all asking for a face pic, which I hadn't uploaded yet. I wanted to know more about who it was I was dealing with before sending any pictures. What if it was someone I knew? The thought horrified me. Two of the messages had face pics and they were both kind of cute. I clicked on their profiles and found out that one was my age and the other much younger. I wasn't sure if I would relate to a younger man, so I messaged back the one my age asking for some more information as the information he sent was somewhat skimpy. I was intrigued, however by the third message. It was a very detailed indicating quite a lot of information about his likes, dislikes, work, education and hobbies. I checked his profile and it was equally detailed. He was quite a bit older than me, but that didn't really bother me as I always felt more comfortable around more mature men. I decided to respond to his message and asked that he give me access to his picture. It wasn't long before I had a notification of a new message from him and when I clicked on it, there was the face pic. Wow! He was some cute. Very distinguished in a mature way with a lovely smile. I sent a message back complimenting him on his good looks and asking that he contact me by email, which I gave him. If I was going to trade pics, I would prefer to do it by email rather than having one on this site, especially after Debbie had told her about a similar site being hacked recently. I checked the profile of the fourth one I selected, but it didn't seem to be what I was looking for. I would wait now for responses to the two messages I had answered.

It wasn't long before I got an email from the older gentleman:

Hi Hotcountrywife. Thank you the compliment and for giving me your email address. It is a lot easier to communicate here than on the site. There was not a lot of information on your profile, so I would like to know more about you; why you are here for one, although I think it is likely for the same reason everyone is. I would also like a picture of you so that I can put a face to the person I am messaging. Also, a name would be nice. David

I looked through the pics on my iPhone and tried to select the best one. I've been told often how attractive I am, but I always hate my pictures because something isn't right in them. I selected one that Peter took in the back yard a few months ago and Air-Dropped it to my iPad. I composed a message and sent it back to him with the picture attached:

Hi David. My name is Angela and I am here, as you say, for the same reason everyone is. I have been married for 20 years…and I don't want to change that…but my husband does not pay the attention to me that I need. I am new to this and still not sure if it is something that I can go through with, so please be patient with me. I have attached a picture taken a few months ago; I hope you like it. Angie.

I didn't want to reveal my husband's addiction issues nor his abuse. I felt that doing so would be a betrayal to him, even though what I was thinking of doing was certainly a betrayal. I wondered again if I could do this. I see-sawed back and forth with the moral issues, yet kept coming back to my needs and my conversations with Debbie. It was only a few minutes before a new message came on my phone and I noticed it was from David. I had opted to have any messages from my 'clandestine' account forwarded to my personal account. Debbie had told me that this is a good way to know when you have a new message in your 'bad girl' account, but to delete them right away and go on-line to read them. I did as she suggested and deleted the message and logged on to my other account.

Wow Angie! You are one attractive lady! It is so nice that when you find some promising contact that she turns out to be gorgeous. I guess combined with your compliment on my photo we have cleared the first hurdle…lol. I would certainly like to meet you in order to clear the second hurdle: Chemistry. It would also be a good opportunity to learn more about each other. When and where would you be able to meet? David xo

Well. That was a nice compliment. God! Now he wants to meet, but then so do I. Where can we meet that no one will see us? My stomach was churning with nervous tension as I wondered what it is I was getting myself into. I needed to talk to Debbie again, so I texted her and asked if she was free for lunch, which she responded right away in the positive.

"So?" She said with raised eyebrows. "Any good prospects yet?"

"Well, yes," I responded somewhat shyly. "There's this one gentleman who intrigued me, but he wants to meet now."

"Of course he wants to meet. Are you going to have cyber-sex or real sex?"

I chuckled at her response.

"Tell me all about him," she said.

"Well, I don't know a lot about him. He is considerably older than I am but real cute."

"Great. Do you have a pic to show me?"

I logged onto the Website and selected the message where he let me access his picture, then turned the phone to her.

"Very nice!" She said with raised eyebrows. "I agree that he is some cute. I had a short fling with an older man once and it was great. I found him more respectful and very experienced in the art of pleasing a woman. Sadly, he moved away and we had to cut it off."

"Where do you suggest we meet? I don't want to risk being seen."

"There are lots of places. Downtown underground parking lots, but I wouldn't recommend that for a first meeting for security reasons. There are lots of hotels or motels that have parking lots hidden from the road. A good one for you would be the Slumber Inn just off the 417."

"OK, I will suggest that. I'm really nervous about the whole thing."

"The nerves will quieten down once you meet him. I'm sure he will be able to put you at ease. Don't forget, it is just a meeting."

"I know, but it is the reason for the meeting that makes me nervous."

We finished our lunch and caught up on other girl things and I went back to the office. I didn't want to reply to his message until I got home and did so from the security of my iPad. Strangely enough, even though

I had not met David yet, he consumed my thoughts as I tried to focus on what I was doing. I realized that amongst the trepidation was an equal amount of excitement. The thought of having a man's arms around me; kissing me all over; fondling me between my legs; being inside me. I shattered the thoughts and got back to my work, looking forward more to going home than I had in a long while so that I could send my message to him.

I was able to get home early, before Peter, and went straight to my room and logged onto my email. I responded to David's message:

Hi David. Thank you very much for the kind words on my photo. I didn't realize it was a hurdle race...lol. Yes, I would love to meet you, but am concerned about being seen. I know that the Slumber Inn just off 417 has a parking lot in the rear and may be a good place to meet. I have flexible hours at work and the morning would be best for me. Let me know what day you want to meet and I will adjust my schedule accordingly. Angie.

I went back to the Website to see if there was any more interesting messages, but I did it half-heartedly because I was excited about seeing how things played out with David. I selected his profile again and clicked on his picture. The more I looked at it the more attracted I became to him. I started to enlarge the picture and study the contours of his face, the colour of his eyes, that wonderful smile with almost-perfect teeth. He had short hair that was very well groomed and he was clean-shaven. He had a very intelligent look about him and I found myself getting wet just imagining those lips on mine. I placed my hand between my legs and started to manipulate myself with my fingers. I was aroused by just looking at his picture for Christ's sake! How was I going to feel when I am next to him? I reached inside my panties and placed my fingers between the folds of flesh to feel the wetness of my pussy. I gently massaged my clitoris while imagining him fondling my body.

"Honey I'm Home!" Peter shouted as he came in the door.

"Shit!" I said to myself. I quickly logged off and composed myself.

"Be right there," I said. I would have to finish this later…

Supper was quiet and Peter said he had to go out with his buddies. I knew he would likely come home drunk, so I said; "Make sure you get a cab or have someone drive you if you are drinking."

"Whatever," he said with a wave of his hand as though to dismiss me.

"Peter!" I said angrily. "What you do in your own time is up to you. I don't care if you drink yourself silly. I really don't. But if you endanger anyone else by driving while you are intoxicated, then I will do something about it."

"So what do you intend to do about it?" He sneered.

"I'm going to have an ignition lock installed on your truck that you won't be able to activate if you are inebriated."

"The fuck you will. Who says you are my keeper?"

"I feel a civic duty to protect others from your careless and thoughtless actions."

"Are you fucking kidding me, Mother Theresa? You just leave my truck alone."

"Promise me you will not drive it while drunk and I will."

"Go to hell!" He said and stomped out.

"Son of a bitch!" I said to myself. Why should I allow myself to be verbally abused like this?

I went to my room and opened my iPad. There was a new message from David:

Hi Angie. I know the place you are referring to and that would work fine for me. I am also quite flexible time-wise, so the morning would work for me. How about 8:00 a.m. tomorrow? Hope I am not rushing things, but I'm really excited about meeting you. Let me know. David. xoxo

I messaged back:

That sounds fine David...and I don't think you are rushing things. In fact I am flattered that you are eager to meet me. I must admit that I am both intrigued and excited about meeting you. How will I recognize your car? I drive a grey 2013 Toyota Camry. Angie. xx

Now I was really excited. I was actually going to meet him tomorrow. I accessed his photo again and gazed at the handsome face...a face I was going to see in the flesh tomorrow. I felt my arousal mounting again and I decided to undress completely. I lay on the bed with my iPad next to me propped up so that I could ogle his photo. I started caressing myself again as my fingers slid effortlessly over the lubricated surface of my clitoris. With my other hand I fondled my breasts and erect nipples. I didn't hold back my emotions and this time didn't stifle my cries. My pelvis arched to the rhythms of my fingers as the first wave of my orgasm started. I plunged my fingers into myself and fondled my G-spot as I continued to stare at David's face. I imagined his mouth on mine and that my fingers were his penis. I exploded in a wonderful orgasm that was more intense than I have experienced in a while. I lay exhausted and so pleased with myself. Hell! If masturbating at his picture can feel this good, I'm certainly looking forward to doing it for real.

I awoke early the next morning and checked my email messages right away. My heart fluttered as I noticed there was one from David:

Hey Angie. That's great...and I am certainly excited about meeting you. I drive a 2013 white Lexus. See you there. David xoxo.

I took a shower and washed my hair. As I toweled myself dry, I looked outside and Peter's truck wasn't there, but I did hear him come home late. Maybe he listened to me after all. It was going to be hot today, so I chose to wear Capri pants and a top that had the lowest neckline I had showing ample cleavage...God! I was actually trying to make myself sexually attractive, something I haven't done since I was dating. But this was kind of a date, wasn't it? I went easy on the make-up; I know that it is a turn-off for some men. I chose a pair of open-toed shoes with a small heel and dried my hair. As I emerged from my bedroom I could hear Peter in the kitchen…I was a little anxious about confronting him as I was in no mood for a fight. He met me with one of his captivating smiles.

"Good morning Honey," he said cheerily. I could smell the bacon as it permeated through the kitchen and dining room. "I made some breakfast. Want some?"

Now that was unusual. Peter was not very adept at any form of cooking, although he was alone for some time before we were married.

"Smells good," I commented as the toast popped up. "Want me to butter that?"

"Sure. How many eggs, one or two?"

"Just one will be fine."

I wanted to ask him what time he came home, but didn't want to bring up that issue in the conversation. He seemed to be in a good mood and I wasn't about to change that. I buttered the toast and set it on the plates. I reached into the cupboard for some jam and placed it on the table. I noticed that there were two steaming cups of coffee already there.

"Anything I can help with?" I asked.

"No thanks. Just sit down and I will be right with you."

He placed an egg on a plate and I heard him say "shit". He scooped out the other two eggs and placed a few strips of bacon next to them.

"Broke an egg," he said sheepishly, but I noticed he had put the broken egg on his own plate.

"This is very nice," I commented as I unfolded my napkin.

He looked at me somewhat sheepishly.

"Look," he said. "About last night"

That's OK," I said. "No need to explain. I see you didn't drive the truck home."

"No, I didn't. Thought about what you said and realized you are absolutely right. It's just that when I drink, it never enters my mind how dangerous it is to drive, so Brent drove me home. He never drinks much and stops long before he has to drive."

"That's good. I hate to be a nag about it."

"No Baby. I don't think you are a nag. I just wish...well...I just wish things were better between us. I know my addictions make things hard for you, but I'm going to try hard to change."

I smiled at him, but it is a replay from what he has said before. He always gives this "I'm going to change" in the morning after the night before. Maybe this time he will mean it.

I looked at the kitchen clock...it was almost 7:30...gotta get going.

"Can you drive me to the bar where I left my truck?"

Shit! I didn't think of that. Of course he will need a drive to get his truck. This will probably make me late for my appointment with David.

"Sure," I said nervously. "Where is it?"

"In Gatineau."

Double shit! This will definitely make me late. It's at least a half-hour's drive from here and that's not counting heavy traffic.

"OK. Are you ready to go now?"

"Sure. After I clean up the kitchen."

"No need to do that. I can do it later."

"I can do it," he said. "Won't take long."

"No. I insist. You were good enough to make breakfast. Only fair that I clean up."

"Do you have to be at work?"

"No!" I said a little too quickly. "Well, yes, I do, but no specific time."

We piled most of the dishes in the dishwasher and left everything else to clean up later. I had to get a message to David to let him know I'm going to be late.

"Just going to get my purse. You can wait for me in the car."

I went into my bedroom and grabbed the phone, logged on to my email and sent a message to David:

Running late, but will be there as soon as I can. Angie xx

I stuffed my phone into my purse, grabbed my car keys, set the alarm and got into my car.

"Now," I said. "Where the hell did you leave your truck?"

* * * *

My phone dinged and I realized it was probably David responding

"Was that yours?" said Peter.

"Yes, probably nothing important. Can't check it while I'm driving."

"Want me to check it for you?"

"No." God! No, I thought. "It's probably one of the health sites I subscribe to, or one of my girlfriends with the latest Internet page going around."

I dropped Peter off at the bar and checked the time; 8:02. Damn! I was at least 30 minutes away from my rendezvous, what with the morning traffic. I checked the message on my phone and it was from David:

No worries...I'm running a little late myself. Have to get gas too. David xoxox

I was a nervous wreck! My stomach was in knots and I now had to go to the bathroom…and I was late! Peter was so sweet this morning and I felt badly about actually meeting another man. But I wasn't going to have sex with him now and it probably isn't going anywhere anyway. I decided to take a breath and slow down…I told him I was going to be late and he acknowledged that.

I pulled into the hotel parking lot, but went to the attached restaurant first to use their bathroom. I still had knots in my stomach, but convinced myself to go through with it. I left the restaurant and drove around to the back of the hotel. There were very few cars in the lot and I noticed his white Lexus right away. I nervously pulled up beside his car and glanced over at him and smiled. He smiled back. Wow! He certainly was easy on the eyes. He got out of his car and walked around to my window.

"Hi Angie," he said. "I must say that you look even better than you did in your photo."

I'm sure I must have blushed a little as I said, "thank you. Sorry I'm late."

"That's OK…so glad you were able to make it. Your car or mine?" He said.

"You seem to have a little more room in yours."

He opened my door and extended a hand to me, which I took and got out. Then he opened the back door of his car.

"I think the front seat would be better," I said. I felt that a console dividing us would keep things proper for a while."

"Absolutely," he said as he opened the front door and I climbed in. "It's just that the back seat has privacy screens, but if you're OK with the front, that's fine with me." I sensed that his eyes were not on my face as he closed the door. He went around the car and got into the driver's side.

"You are absolutely gorgeous," he said as he turned to face me. Again, I noticed his eyes lowering to my cleavage, which made me smile smugly.

I thanked him again and wanted to return the compliment, but thought better of it. I wanted to see where this was going before I 'encouraged' him. I had to admit though that he was very handsome with a pleasant smile and perfect teeth…he could have been in a Colgate ad. He was dressed casually in a golf shirt and matching sports pants. I could smell whatever fragrance he used…either his underarm deodorant or maybe aftershave mixed with a pleasant-smelling soap…competing with the leather smell from the car.

"So," he said. "Nervous?"

"You bet," I said. "I've never done this before and my stomach right now is in knots."

"That's natural…hopefully we can ease those knots."

I smiled at him and he reached over and gently took my hand in his. It felt so nice.

"Tell me a little more about yourself," he asked.

"Not much to tell. I've been married for 20 years and have two lovely children…I guess they're not children any more. They are both away at University and it's just my husband and me now at home. We live just out of town on a small hobby farm. I have a dog, two cats and some chickens. That's about it."

"So, I can see where the 'Hotcountrywife' came in," he said with a smile.

"Oh, that was my friend's idea."

"Do you share such things with your friends?"

"Only the one. We have been very close for many years and pretty well reveal everything to each other. Don't worry, she's not about to tell anyone about us because she is cheating on her husband too. She is the one who suggested the Website and helped me create the profile. I am new to all this and she helped me with security issues."

"That's good. Security is an issue and I'm glad that someone has given you some pointers on keeping things discrete. So, tell me why you are on the site."

I wasn't sure that I was prepared to spill my guts on my marital situation to a stranger, so I said:" My husband doesn't pay the attention to me that I need. I am a passionate person and feel that something is missing in that department. I think I need to have someone want me, not for sex but for who I am. It's easy for a woman to get laid. Hell! I had upwards of a hundred responses on the site in just a few days. Most of them were garbage though, what with abusive messages and dick pics I ended up deleting most of them."

"Are you messaging or meeting with anyone else?"

"No. I did message with one other person, but declined to meet him."

"I'm flattered," he said.

"You had a nice profile and you seemed to be genuine, so I thought it would be interesting to at least meet with you."

"I'm so glad you did," he said as he covered my hand with his other hand and gently squeezed it. Christ! I was getting aroused and could feel myself getting wet. The knots in my stomach had gone and were now replaced with butterflies. I felt my breathing become shallower just in the presence of this person. He reached over and tried to kiss me. I offered my cheek, but he brought his hand up to my chin and tilted my head towards him. His lips gently brushed mine and I closed my eyes. I could smell the sweetness of his breath and the smell of soap on his skin. His lips were so soft and pliable and seemed to meld with mine as though they were meant to be together. I had never experienced a kiss like this before. Normally, one would pucker up to kiss, but he didn't and neither did I. We just let our mouths explore each other with tender movements and it felt so natural. He stopped kissing me and I realized that I was still posing there until I came out of my trance and opened my eyes.

"That was very nice," he said. "You have very kissable lips."

"You too," I said, but noticed that my speech was not normal because I was finding it hard to breath properly. What was happening to me? I was so wet I felt I should be wearing a tampon! He reached over to kiss me again, but I reluctantly pulled away.

"Look," I said. "This is all very new to me and I need to slow down. I don't know yet if this is something I can do. I need time."

"Take all the time you need," he said. "I'm in no hurry. It's better not to rush these things because if you're not sure, you have to remember it is something you can't undo. Not everyone is cut out to handle the deceit and lies that go with having an affair. If we were to take this to the next step, I want to be sure that it is something you are not going to regret."

I smiled and said: "Thanks for understanding."

We talked some more about general things…his family and kids and why he was doing this. Seems he is being denied sex and hasn't been intimate with his wife in months. He talked about his business and I talked about the farm and my work. I looked at my watch and saw that it was almost 10…we had been talking for an hour and a half.

"Oh! My gosh!" I said. "It's ten o'clock! I need to get to the office."

"Hey!" He said. "Time flies when you're having fun. And I am certainly having fun."

"Me too," I admitted. "It's been very nice talking to you…and thanks for not rushing me."

"You're welcome," he said as he reached his face over to me again. This time, I didn't pull away and he didn't have to angle my face to him. I wanted to feel his lips on mine again. Our lips met and I savored the wondrous feeling it gave me. He didn't try to shove his tongue down my throat, or even use his tongue at all. Just gentle and soft movements that felt so natural. I don't think I have ever been kissed like that before. He broke contact and smiled at me, which I returned.

"I hope I can see you again," he said.

"Probably," was all I could say. I didn't want to lead him on, but knew the answer was yes.

"Good enough for me," he said and opened his door, then came around the car and opened the passenger door. He offered his hand, which I accepted and he helped me out of the car. Once I was out, he opened my door and I got into my own car, then closed the door. I was feeling so...'ladylike'...with his chivalry and gentlemanly gestures. I was also conscious again of his eyes on my cleavage, and I felt OK with that. I wound down my window as I started the car. He reached his head in the window and gave me another superb kiss.

"A la prochain," he said as he stepped away from the car. I reversed out of the parking stall and placed the car in drive. He waved at me as I pulled away and I waved back. The butterflies were still there as I pulled out of the parking lot and headed to the office. Somehow, I felt very satisfied with myself and was sure that we were going to meet again.

THREE

We had exchanged cell phone numbers and he reminded me to password-protect my phone, but showed me how to access it with the thumbprint on the select button. He also said that once the text is read to delete it, which made sense. I hadn't even reached my office when I got a text message. I didn't want to access it while driving, but I couldn't wait to read it. I pulled into the nearest parking lot and opened my phone:

You are amazing! Thanks for the wonderful kisses…left me wanting for more. xoxo

I smiled and responded:

You are very welcome. You are pretty special too. Thanks for making me feel sexy again. xxx

With that I pulled out of the parking lot and proceeded to the office. I texted Deborah:

Meeting went well. He is very nice.

Immediately came the response:

Great Kiddo. Lunch?

I smiled as I knew she would be busting at the seams for all the details, so I wrote:

Sure.

"So," Deborah said excitedly. "Tell me all about it…and I want to know all the sordid details."

"There are no sordid details," I said, then proceeded to tell her about our general conversation. Seems she wasn't really interested in the general conversation. But more the connection.

"So, how do you feel about him?"

"What do you mean 'how do I feel about him'?"

"Did he kiss you?"

"Yes."

"Come on, do I have to drag it out of you? How was it?"

"It was the most amazing kiss I have ever experienced," I said somewhat dreamily.

Deborah pumped her fist and said: "Yes!"

"So," she continued. "When do you see him again?"

"I don't know. We haven't established anything yet."

"What!" She said incredulously. "You've just met a man who gave you the best kiss in your life," she accentuated 'life', "and you haven't made a date for another meeting? For heaven's sake, don't let him get away."

"He isn't getting away." I said. "I wanted to take it slowly and he understood."

"You are going to see him again Angie. Tell me you are going to see him again."

"I just don't know yet. Yes, I want to see him again. He really turns me on. But that's what bothers me. Peter was so sweet this morning and apologetic. He even made breakfast. I don't know if I can do this to him. In spite of his addiction problems, I do love him and if I cheat on him I know I'm going to regret it."

"Listen Angie. I know what you are going through because I was experiencing the same dilemma. But things just didn't change. Yes, I felt some regret and remorse after the first time. But every time things flared up again at home, I longed for my lover and the regret and remorse eventually went away."

We finished our lunch and I went back to work. I logged on to the Cheating Spouses site from my phone and looked at his profile. His profile page showed he had logged on within the last hour. I felt a twinge in my stomach. Was he still looking? I guess I had not given any assurances to

30

him about seeing him again, so why wouldn't he keep looking? I had another new feeling I hadn't experienced for a long time. Jealousy! What if he found someone else? I said I didn't want to rush into things but knew that I would be upset if he chose someone else. All these emotions were new to me and although exciting, they did cause some consternation.

When I got home, there was an email message waiting for me from David. I excitedly opened it and read it:

Hi Angie. I really enjoyed our time together today. I realize that you want to go slow, but I must admit that I am smitten with you. I want you to know that I am not seeing or even meeting with anyone else at the moment. In fact, I closed my profile today as a sign of good faith to show you that I am not rushing you and am prepared to wait until I get a definite no from you before opening it again. I want you Angie and am prepared to wait for you. Love. David xoxoxo

Well, what a lovely message…and that would explain him being on the site earlier today. I thought for a while and composed my response. I deleted the message from my personal mail folder and logged on to my other email:

Hi David. I also enjoyed our time together today. Thank you for making me feel sexy again and wanted. Thank you also for closing your profile and I am going to do the same. Be assured that if I decide to go ahead with this, I can think of no better person to do so with. Please be patient…I can promise you that it could be very rewarding… ☺ Angie. xxxx

The butterflies had returned to my stomach. I logged off of my email and logged on to the 'Cheating Spouses' Website. There were over 60 messages waiting in my inbox. I went to the 'Profile' page and selected 'Delete Profile' and clicked the button. After the message, 'Do you really want to delete your profile? You have unread messages in your inbox. All information associated with this profile will be deleted'. I pressed 'Yes' and closed the program. I wasn't even interested in reading the new messages that were there. I was sure that David would be the one with whom I would take this journey. I closed the Safari browser and noticed a new message in my mailbox. I still had my other mailbox open so went there to read it:

Thank you for the kind words...I'm glad that you felt it too...that 'connection'. You can bet that I am going to be patient, but it is going to be painful. They say that good things come to those who wait and I know in this case 'they' are right. I have been on this site for some time and have only met with a few women and only slept with one. It didn't work out and we only did it once. I am not here to put notches on my bedpost...far from it. I know what I am looking for and know I have found it. I just hope that you can figure all this out in your mind and agree to meet with me again. If you are not comfortable with meeting behind closed doors yet, I'm OK with that too. Love. David xoxoxo

I smiled when I read it. I somehow felt that I would very soon work all this out in my mind and meet with him again...and it will be behind closed doors.

* * * * *

The house phone rang and I picked it up.

"Hello."

"Angela Davenport?"

"Yes. Who is this?"

"This is Sergeant Dickens of the Ottawa Police. We have your husband in custody here for a DUI. He is being charged with driving while over the legal limit of alcohol. We will be holding him in a cell for overnight while he sobers up. Did you wish to come and pick him up tomorrow?"

I was shocked. He didn't listen after all. God! I was so angry.

"Yes," I stammered. "I will be there tomorrow."

"Any time after 9 a.m.," he said. "His truck is in the police pound and it will be kept there for a week. There will, of course, be a charge of $50 per day to retrieve it, which is a minimum of $350."

"Thanks," I said and hung up the phone. "Fuck!" I said out loud. I was fuming. Now he was being charged for driving while intoxicated as well as accruing charges for getting his truck out of the pound. I reflected on Debbie's comment about things not changing…and she was right. Things weren't going to change with Peter until he agrees to attend AA meetings and so far, he has refused to do so. I just can't go on like this…the drunken sessions and abuse and the repentance next morning. It made me think about David and somehow, both my reluctance to meet with him and remaining faithful to Peter was very quickly fading.

I tried to watch a movie on TV after supper but couldn't get into it. I had fleeting images of Peter laying in a cell and then images of David laying on top of me. My mind went from anger to erotic pleasures and back again. I finally fell asleep on the couch with a smile on my face thinking of David.

I awoke and I had made up my mind then and there what I was going to do. I wondered about what to wear…something that is easily removed? I went through my underwear drawer and selected the sexiest bra and panties I could find, which was not really very sexy as I had no real need for such things lately. I decided to wear jeans and a top. I arrived at the police station at 9:15 and asked for Sergeant Dickens. I stated my name and Peter's name saying I was there to pick him up.

"The sergeant will be right with you," said the receptionist." If you would take a seat over there?" she pointed to some seats over by the wall. I was so embarrassed just to be here sitting amongst a questionable array of Ottawa's miscreants. I decided to stand. After 10 minutes or so a door next to the receptionist opened and a uniformed man stepped out. He looked at me and said: "Ms. Davenport?"

"Yes, that's me." I was going to correct him and say "Mrs." but decided not to.

"Please step this way," he said motioning towards the door he had just stepped through. I followed him down a long hallway with offices on each side and he showed me through an open door into a sparse room where Peter sat at a table. He looked at me with sorrow on his face.

"I'm so sorry Angie," he said with tears in his eyes. I just said: "Come, let's just get the hell out of here!"

We walked back through the corridor and out into the parking lot, not saying anything. We drove home in silence…I didn't speak and Peter knew enough not to with the look of anger on my face.

* * * * *

I went home and let him out at the front door.

"How am I going to get to work?" He said.

"Quite frankly, I don't give a fuck?" I said. "Call a cab or get one of your buddies to drive you. You're going to be without your truck for at least a week and could end up with a license suspension when your case comes up in court"

With that I stormed off spinning gravel from the front tires as I sped off down the laneway. I glanced in the rearview mirror and saw Peter just standing there. Good! I thought to myself. Let him stew for a while.

When I got to work I immediately logged on to my email from my phone and composed a message to David:

Hi David. I have thought a lot about whether we should see each other again. I have very conflicting emotions about it, but each time I come back to the memories of those kisses, I know I have to do this for myself. I'm going to very nervous, but I know what we will be meeting for, so…find a room, today! Before I change my mind. Angie xxx

I pressed 'send' before I changed my mind. "There, it's done." I said to myself. It wasn't long before I received a reply:

That's absolutely wonderful Angie. You have made me a very happy man. I have made a reservation at the Slumber Inn for today…seems somewhat fitting. I was thinking sometime in the afternoon, or we can meet any time before tomorrow's check-out time of 11 a.m., so tomorrow morning could also work. Can't wait to get some more of those awesome kisses. Love, David. xoxox

I replied:

This afternoon is fine. Meet you there at 2 p.m. I have some other questions though. What about condoms? I am not on any birth control at the moment and we have to consider safe sex, don't we? Angie. xxx

My phone dinged with a new message:

Good questions Angie and they should be addressed. No need to worry about getting pregnant as I have had a vasectomy. As for the safe sex issue, I am not having sex with anyone and neither are you, so we can't infect each other. However, I will leave the decision to you. I will bring a condom just in case. David. xoxox

I couldn't resist responding:

Only one…lol

When the new message signal sounded I read it:

Lol. I'll bring the whole box!

I was in a great mood now. I wanted to do it today while I was in the frame of mind I was. I was afraid that if I waited, I would revert to my guilty sense and not see him. Right now the butterflies in my stomach were rampant and I felt like I was walking on air. I was tempted to text Deborah and let her know but decided against it…I would tell her all about it afterwards. I watched the clock as it slowly crept around the face and found it hard to concentrate on my work, what with trips to the bathroom! When it got to one o'clock, I decided to leave the office and take a late lunch at the restaurant by the motel…I wasn't going to be late again.

As I sat there finishing my meal I saw David's car pull into the motel driveway and go around to the back. I wondered if he would notice that my car was already there. I then saw him walk around to the front entrance and go inside. It wasn't long before I got a text message:

Room 212. Did I see your car in the parking lot?

I smiled at his observance:

Yes, very observant of you. I decided to come here for lunch. Be right there.

My phone dinged again:

Just habit. I always check the cars when I get into a parking lot for any I recognize…lol.

Smart, I thought. I crossed the driveway to the motel entrance casting furtive glances around for anyone I might know. It's interesting that one cannot hide the fact that what you are doing is wrong and that you are out of your comfort zone. It was sunny and hot that day and at least I could wear my sunglasses in a veiled attempt to disguise my identity. Once I was in the motel I casually strolled past the reception without glancing at the receptionist and entered the elevator…I pressed '2' for the second level. As I stepped out of the elevator, my heart was racing as I walked up to the door. I hesitated, poised with my clenched fist, afraid to knock. I rapped lightly on the door…he probably didn't hear that, I thought to myself…so I prepared to knock again when the door opened. He was standing there, smiling at me and I just stood there…afraid to move. He reached out his hand to me and said, "It's going to be OK". I took his hand and he led me into the room. I casually glanced at the bed and my heart was in my throat. Am I really going to do this? He put his arms around me and we hugged for what seemed like an eternity, but probably only a few minutes. We broke the embrace and he looked at me.

"You're gorgeous," he said. I coyly responded with a "thank you". "These are for you," He said pointing to a beautiful bouquet of flowers in a crystal vase sitting on the dresser.

"Thank you again," I said, admiring the array of colours and the fresh smell, thinking what I was going to do with them as I couldn't take them home.

Angela's Seduction

He placed his hand under my chin and tilted my head up to him. We kissed. A long, soft and gentle kiss, just like those we did in the car a lifetime ago. Lips brushing…exploring…tantalizing. I inhaled the aroma of him and it was intoxicating. I could feel my excitement rising and the knots in my stomach were receding. I had sensations between my legs that I had not felt in some time. I felt the tip of his tongue as it circled my lips, so I parted my lips and met his tongue with mine. We played for a while with our tongues…exploring…seeking…gently feeling each other's moistness. Speaking of which, I could feel my own moistness now and I could also feel his hardness as he pressed against me. Our kisses became deeper…more passionate…tongues dancing feverishly.

We moved towards the bed…which was good because my legs were about to collapse under me…and he reached down and lifted my top. I reached my arms upwards so that he could take it off completely. I coyly stood there in my bra…it's been a while since another man has seen me like this. He reached down and kissed the side of my face; my neck; my shoulders; then placed a kiss on the top of each breast.

"You have beautiful breasts," he said. "I'm sure you sensed me looking at them in the car yesterday".

"Why! I do declare," I said in my best Southern accent, flashing my eyelashes. "Yo all been starin' at my lil' ol' boobies. Shame on you sir."

He laughed and then turned me around and kissed the top of my shoulders; my back...his hands caressing me as he did so. I felt his hands reach for my bra clasp to undo it and I let it fall to the floor, embarrassingly covering myself with my hands. His hands reached around to my front and removed mine from my breasts, replacing them with his. God! His hands felt so good as he manipulated my erect nipples with his fingers, all the while kissing my back lower and lower. I felt so wonderful and closed my eyes to fully enjoy this heavenly attention. The feeling of his hands, mouth and tongue on my body made me tingle all over. He moved his hands from my breasts to my belt buckle, undid it and pulled down the zipper of my jeans, then pulled them down. As I stepped out of them, I could feel his kisses now as he moved increasingly further down my body…my ass, the top of my legs down to the back of my knees.

He turned me around and brought his head up to my breasts and gently kissed each one in turn, his hands simultaneously sliding up the inside of my leg. He touched me there…Oh! My God! It felt so good as he gently massaged me while suckling on my nipples, each one in turn. He guided me to the bed and I sat down on the edge, then he eased me back and I lay down, my legs dangling over the edge. Reaching for my legs, he lifted them up and started kissing my feet, sucking on my toes, then working down each leg in turn…first the ankles, calves, lower leg and upper thighs. His lips and tongue traced a path inside my thighs as they honed in on the treasured spot between them. I could feel him licking me at the top of my legs…each side of my pussy…I was so turned on now…more than I can remember in a long time…if ever. What this amazing person was doing to me was so rapturous I wanted to surrender completely to him. Finally, he was there…his mouth cupped the flesh through the panties and it was ecstatic. My breathing was now quickening as I felt him manipulate the folds of flesh beneath. He then reached for the waistband and peeled the panties off as I raised my butt. He tossed then somewhere but I was not about to wonder where. I wanted his mouth on me again…and then it was there. I could feel the soft and warm wetness of his tongue as it sought out my clitoris; my arousal heightened now to a point where I knew a climax was imminent. His arms folded around my legs and he clasped his hands on my stomach – locked in place. I was in a dream…my whole concentration on what he was doing to me...the World could end now and I wouldn't know it. I could feel his tongue alternating from circular to up-and-down to side-to side motions. He moved down and inserted his tongue into my vagina, thrusting it in and out, then back to the manipulations of my clitoris. I then felt his whole mouth on me, enveloping my labia as he sucked on them and rolled them around in his mouth. I was almost there, the feelings mounting inside of me like a volcano about to erupt. He reached for my hands and I clasped them tightly as the wave of ecstasy was about to enfold me. I teetered on the edge for just a moment…then exploded in a violent orgasm that shook me all over. I convulsed with each involuntary spasm, unable to stifle my cries. It seemed like it would never end, but eventually I returned to a normal state, totally spent, as though all my energy had been channeled to that one orgasm.

"Wow!" He said. "That was a good one."

"Wonderful" was all I was able to utter in my breathless state.

He got to his feet and started to undress…shirt, jeans, underwear, socks. He stood there naked, his erect member tantalizing me as I stared at it. I had not been very keen on performing oral sex on a man in the past; but I wanted it in my mouth…

I positioned myself fully on the bed and he lay down beside me. We hugged and kissed as I sought out his manhood with my hands. God! It felt so good…so firm, yet silky soft to the touch. I rolled over and straddled him, then moved my head down and kissed his neck, chest and stomach, gently stroking his manhood as I did so. His skin felt so smooth to my mouth and tongue and I reveled in his sighs of appreciation…and then I was there! I inhaled the musty scent of him...clean with that mild trace of perspiration. I brushed my lips on the crown…it felt so firm yet velvety soft to the touch. I turned my face and rubbed him on my cheeks; my nose; my eyes…everywhere on my face. I gently kissed the glans all over, then dry-mouthed it as I listened to his moans of pleasure. I inserted my tongue into his urethra and then flicked the frenulum with it...which I have to say elicited quite a reaction. I mouthed the shaft along its length and cupped his testicles in my hand and kissed them too. I moved down to the top of his legs and licked between them…long strokes beside his testicles on each side of them. Then I worked my way up again and this time, took him fully in my mouth and circled the head with my tongue. I was so enamoured with what I was doing and the incredible attraction I had to his penis. I sucked down on it and then moved my head back up to the top, circling the crown again with my tongue. I repeated this motion several times until he stopped me, saying "You're going to finish me too quickly".

I smiled at him and sat up, then put my leg over and straddled him. I eased myself down so that I touched his hardness with my pussy, then eased back and forth on a film of abundant lubricant, caressing him with my labia. I looked down and could see the head protrude as I moved backwards, only to see it disappear on my forward movements. I was kneading his chest with my hands as I watched the look of pleasure on his face. I eased myself up and stood him up...then impaled myself on him. We both groaned in ecstasy. He was now fully inside of me and it felt heavenly. I had not experienced very many men before and David was certainly above average in size...at least what I considered as average. I did not move for a while as I contracted my vaginal muscles to squeeze him. As I did this, I could feel his hardness pulse in response. After a few moments, I lifted myself up until he was almost out, squeezed the crown with my vaginal muscles, and then plunged down once more. I contracted my muscles on the upward stroke and released then on the down stroke. I knew he was close, as was I to my second orgasm. He stopped me just as he was about to explode and I dismounted.

He reached for my ass and guided my body up his. I lifted my legs over his arms and lowered myself onto his mouth. He lifted each of his legs in turn and guided my arms to encircle them for support, then stuck out his tongue and motioned me to manipulate myself on him. I got the idea and moved my body so that his tongue could pleasure me there. Wow! This was so good as I was able to control my own pleasure. I started with my clitoris, then my vagina, labia, every part of that treasured spot. My movements became faster; more aggressive; I felt I may hurt him but the pleasure was so great I'm sure he would let me know if I did. It did not take long before I reached another climax and I cupped his face in my hands.

"Arhh!" I cried with each wave, convulsing uncontrollably and crushing my pussy into his face. "Arhh!...Arhhh!"

When I had finished, I stayed there for a minute or two collecting myself while he gently tongued my pussy. I watched him with admiration and adoration, my hands still cradling his head and my fingers twirling through his hair. I was amazed at the incredible feelings this man was giving me. When I eventually dismounted…spent…exhausted…totally sated, he turned me over so that he was now above me, kneeling between my legs. He knelt there momentarily, looking at me, admiring me, fondling me gently with his hands, his member showing his full arousal.

"You are so fucking beautiful," he said as he slowly lay on top of me. I felt his hardness touch me there and I so wanted it inside of me. I closed my eyes to concentrate on the pleasure of it.

"Open your eyes," he said. "I want you to see my pleasure".

I did so and stared into his eyes and saw the adoration in them. He reached his hands down to my butt and lifted it as he inserted himself inside me.

"Ohhh!" I cried.

It felt heavenly as I felt his penis plunge deep into my pussy. God! He felt so good as he slowly pushed it all the way in. We didn't move for a while, savoring the wonderful feeling of closeness and connection while we tenderly kissed. I sensed him withdrawing and I somehow felt disappointment, wondering if he was going to pull all the way out, but before he withdrew completely, he thrust himself back in again.

"Ohhh! Ohhh!" I cried again as he set up a tempo of in and out movements. I could feel his testicles slapping on my ass as he plunged into me, both of us grunting with each thrust. He pumped harder and harder as I contracted and he responded in decreasing time elements. I felt his hard penis turn to granite and I knew he was about to climax. This excited me immensely as I cried out, "Yes! Yes!" I grabbed at his ass and pulled him into me, then he uttered a guttural groan and exploded inside of me. I could feel his ejaculate filling me up and I released again and we pulsed together, tightly grasping at each other and feverishly seeking out each other's mouth. I could smell myself on him and that excited me even more.

We were both spent now…gasping for precious air between tender kisses. He dismounted and we lay there in an embrace…my head on his chest…glistening bodies touching. I could feel his semen leaking out of my pussy and it felt so…satisfying.

"That was absolutely wonderful," he said. "I'm so glad you decided to do this. Are you OK?"

I thought for a moment. I wasn't sure exactly what it was I was feeling. Conflicting thoughts, maybe? I was well sated, that was for sure. I also felt that something that had been missing from my life was now there. Right now, I was feeling absolutely wonderful.

"I'm OK," I said.

FOUR

We got dressed and bade each other goodbye with some more kisses.

"Better that we not leave together," he said as he opened the door. I smiled and gave him one last kiss and left the room. I was walking on air and felt so wonderful that I didn't even think about Peter; only when I was going to see David again. I could still somehow feel him inside me and the butterflies were still there. I got in my car and checked for any phone messages…I had placed it in silent mode while with David. There was a text message from Deborah as well as a few other inconsequential emails. I then went back to the office and responded to Debbie's message, which had simply asked how things were going.

Hi Debbie. Things are going well. Met with David this afternoon and we did it!

I knew that the message would elicit quite a response and she would want to meet to hear all about it. Sure enough, my phone dinged and it was her:

Holy shit Angie! You actually had sex with him? This is great! Need to see you to hear all about it.

I smiled as she was so predictable. I'm sure that in the same circumstance, I would be the same. I think Debbie somehow feels that she is my coach in this and needs to be kept fully informed. I texted back:

Sure Deborah…see you at Grace O'Malley's at 5.

When I got there at 5 minutes before 5 I knew Debbie would already be there. She stood and waved wildly from one of the rear booths and I acknowledged her with a wave of my own.

She was smiling from ear to ear as I sat in the booth opposite her.

"Angie, you old slut," she said jokingly. "I really didn't think you would do it."

"Not so much of the 'old'," I said with a pout.

"So, tell me all about it," she said excitedly. "I really didn't expect anything to happen so fast."

"I did it more out of impulse because I was so pissed at Peter."

"What did he do now?"

"He got arrested for DUI and spent the night in the slammer."

"Oh for Christ's sake no! I am so sorry Angie. That's terrible. I know that he will likely lose his license and his vehicle will be impounded for a week. I suggest he get some legal advice. Why don't you talk to one of your lawyers? I'm sure you have people who specialize in that and he may be able to get the charges reduced."

"Sure Deborah. I am still so angry at him. I hope that this is the catalyst that gets him to change his ways though."

"I hope so too. So, tell me all about your meeting with David. And…I want *all* the details."

I sat there and recounted the wonderful afternoon I had experienced. I wasn't sure how much detail I was prepared to reveal to Debbie, but I really wanted to shout it out to the World…I felt so good. I realized though that if I didn't at least tell something, I would burst, so I gave a Cole's Notes version.

"Well," I started. "I was so pissed at Peter after hearing about his DUI that I decided to go ahead and meet with David. I said to arrange it for this afternoon before I changed my mind. He was an utter gentleman and man, was he sexy." I stared into space as I recounted the rapturous moments. "His hands felt so wonderful on my body and he kissed me in places I didn't even know I had places. He smelled heavenly and his manhood felt great when I touched it. I don't think I have ever been turned on so much in my life."

When I looked at Debbie, her eyes were like saucers and I could swear she was dribbling.

"Go on," she said. "Did you...like...suck on it?"

"Absolutely," I said, lowering my voice and casting furtive glances around me to see if anyone was within earshot. "And I have never really liked sucking cock before. I even would have taken his cum in my mouth, which amazed me that I would even consider it."

"It's an acquired taste," she said. "But with the right guy, you will get to love it. I have never taken Andy's semen in my mouth...hell, I rarely ever took his dick in my mouth, but with Richard I do it all the time. So, what else?"

"I was so eager to have him inside me and when he was, it was something out of this World."

"Was he...big? Cut or uncut?"

I smiled at Debbie's quest for the sordid details.

"I wouldn't say he was huge...but maybe above average. I haven't seen that many and he is a little larger than Peter. It didn't really matter anyway because he was a master at using it...and, for your information seeing as you need to know...he was cut."

"Does he shave his balls?"

"Deborah!" I said somewhat exasperated.

"Sorry," she said. "I guess I'm trying to picture things in my mind."

"Well, you can picture it however you want to."

She looked at me with her usual pout when she doesn't get her way.

"Yes," I said.

"Awesome," she said as she pumped her fist. "I am so happy for you Kiddo. Just don't start beating up on yourself about it. Best is to separate Peter and David into two separate lives. As long as you keep them apart, then everything will be OK. If and when the remorse and guilt hits, set it aside and think about why you are doing this. On no account feel that you can absolve your guilt and make things right by telling Peter. It will just fuck things up for good. If you decide to stop seeing David, for whatever reason, just keep it to yourself and move on."

"Thanks Deborah, I will remember that. For now things are good and I feel no compulsion to 'tell all' to Peter."

"That's good. So, when are you going to see David again?"

"We didn't make another 'date', so to speak, but I'm sure it will be soon enough."

"Wonderful. I am so happy for you. Especially as I feel responsible for getting you into this."

"Yes, that's right. It is all your fault," I chided and we both laughed.

We finished our drinks and I went home…not anxious to face Peter. I was afraid that I would have guilt written all over my face. I stared through the windshield as the wipers swept intermittently the light rain that was now falling. I chewed on a breath mint to mask the smell of alcohol on my breath, although it really didn't matter. When I got home, I decided to pour myself a sherry anyway as Peter wasn't there and I didn't know how he was getting around. Didn't really care because every time I thought about how stupid he had been, it made me angry. About half an hour later, I heard a car on the gravel driveway and looked out of the window. I saw it was Brian from his work and after Peter got out, he drove off. It was raining heavily now and Peter held his briefcase over his head and ran through the downpour to the side door.

"Honey, I'm home," he shouted as he came in to the kitchen.

"In the living room," I called back.

"Hi," he said as he came into the living room. "Into the drinks already?"

"Things have been a little hectic lately, don't you think?" I didn't want to encourage him to drink and was somewhat guilty of seemingly blaming him for my need to drink.

"Can we talk about it?"

"Sure."

He ambled over to the sofa sat down beside me. He seemed to be composing his thoughts and I waited for him to speak.

"I know that a simple apology isn't enough," he started. "I know also that my actions over the last few days have been…hurtful to you."

He looked at me for some kind of acknowledgement and I said, "I'm listening."

He looked down at the floor, composing his thoughts again. He rubbed his hands together in a nervous manner and then wiped what I presumed to be sweaty palms onto his pants. Peter never was very good at conversation and usually chose his words carefully. Maybe it is a throwback to his military training where one had to be cautious of what you said and to whom you said it.

"I don't want to make excuses…you deserve better than that…but you have to believe that I am trying, but obviously not hard enough."

Took the words right out of my mouth…

I took a sip of my sherry, but did not offer any response. I wanted to hear all he had to say first. He fidgeted nervously, then leaned back in the sofa.

"I'm going to go to the AA meetings you kept insisting on," he finally said. He looked at me for a response and I figured that was what he intended to tell me.

"That's great," I said. "I think it will do you…us…a lot of good." I wanted to say more but felt that it was better at this time to leave it as it is. He had agreed to do it without my further insistence and that was a good thing; he had made the decision.

"There's a meeting tomorrow at 8:00 p.m. at the Holy Cross Church on Walkley and I intend to go."

"Do you want me to come with you?"

"No, if you don't mind. I feel I have to do this on my own. I know you want what's best for me…us, but it's my problem and I need to solve it."

I didn't agree with his logic…it was *our* problem and he wasn't really responsible for it if it is a result of his PTSD. He didn't have the problem before he went to Afghanistan. But Peter has always been more introverted and had issues sharing personal feelings, so I said OK.

I started supper and decide on some lamb chops that Peter would have to BBQ. I knew he liked to BBQ as it always gave him a sense of helping when he was so inept in the kitchen. I prepared some mini-potatoes, sprinkled them with butter and mint leaves and nuked them. It was a warm evening and so we decided to eat outside. Supper was quiet and I tried to find some subject matter to discuss, but Peter was not very talkative, so I gave up and we ate in relative silence.

After clearing away the dishes, we watched a movie on TV and then each went to our own bedrooms. I was anxious to see if there were any messages from David. I logged on to my 'clandestine' email and sure enough, there was a message from David. It's funny how such an event can create such a high level of excitement…just the fact that he was thinking of me and messaging me. I opened the message:

Hi Sweetie. Still thinking about our time together today…you were absolutely magnificent. I know this being the first time you have done this that there must be lots of thoughts going around that pretty little head of yours. I want you to make the right decision and I want that decision to include me. I want to see you again and soon…☺ Affectionately, David xoxox

I read and re-read the message and each time it made my heart race. I had been having thoughts about the whole thing, but one thing was certain, I was going to be seeing David again. I composed a message and wrote back to him:

Angela's Seduction

Hi David. Yes, today was magnificent. There were so many things I liked about today and I don't think I have ever had such a wonderful sexual experience. Yes, I have been doing a lot of soul-searching and thinking about whether I am cut out for an affair, but I don't think I can make that judgement on just one meeting. So, regrettably, we will have to do it again...lol. I can probably get away next week sometime, so whenever it is convenient for you, we can meet again. Love, Angie xxx

I read it over several times before I pressed 'send'. I didn't want to overthink the whole thing and find things wrong with what we were doing, although clearly it was wrong...I just didn't want to find reasons not to do it.

Less than 15 minutes later, the reply came in:

Hey Baby. Yes, I agree that you should do it again, and again, and again...lol. You've made me a happy man and we can certainly meet next week. I am very flexible and so, I understand, are you, so it should not be a problem meeting. How about Tuesday, same place, same time? Love, David xoxox

* * * * *

We did meet again as planned, but this time my nervous apprehension was replaced with carnal desire...I just couldn't wait to get at his body again and feel his hands on me. Growing up in a small-town environment I was never exposed to sex until I met Peter. He too was from a farm and from what I could gather, had very little sexual experience as well. We were like two novices finding our way and doing for the most part what came naturally. We tried oral sex early in our relationship, but it seemed that neither of us were adept at it and so we just left it at that. Peter and I had known each other since we were in school and I guess he was considered as my high school sweetheart. We dated other people off and on but always gravitated back to each other. We became more companions than lovers and it seemed like a foregone conclusion that we would eventually marry. Life was orchestrated in that we made babies and satisfied our parents and did

49

all the things we were supposed to do. Sex was taboo in our family and I can't even imagine my father fucking my mother, but I guess they did since there was me and I had two brothers.

While in college, some of the dorm residents would have 'porn' parties where someone would rent a video player and somehow get hold of a copy of some porn movie. Of course, in the early 90s, access to porn was not quite like it is now. I remember when a classmate invited me to one of these parties and it was all women. They had a copy of "Deep Throat" and I was horrified by what I saw. But what surprised me the most was that I was very much turned on by it. The girls would hoot and holler when Linda Lovelace would take a 13" cock down her throat. I had never seen pictures of other women's pussies either and the sight of that I found stimulating. I was embarrassed at the feelings I was having and quickly dispelled them as 'wrong' or 'inappropriate'.

I was about to leave home to meet David at the prescribed time of 2:00 p.m. I had decided to work from home because much of what I wanted to do was just some administration. I set the alarm and closed the front door and went to my car…only to be met by about half a dozen chickens.

"Fuck!" I said out loud. "Just what I need right now." I could see that a part of the chicken coop's fence was broken, so I had to round up the stray hens in my high-heeled shoes. As I darted around the yard shooing them back to the coop I was concerned that I was going to be late again to meet David. I was able to get them all back in and made a temporary repair to the fencing, but I realized that I had mud over my shoes. I went into the house through the back door and the alarm went off!

"Fuck!" I said out loud again. I silenced the alarm on the keypad and went to the closet to get a cloth to clean my shoes over the slop sink. The phone rang and I was hesitant to answer it, but I thought it might be the alarm company, so I did, and it was. I gave my password and hung up, then looked at the clock. Christ! It was 1:55 and I had a 20-minute drive. I figured David would likely be at or near the motel, so I called him on his cell.

"Hi Sweetie," he said.

"Hi David. I'm late again. Had to round up some stray chickens, then I tripped the alarm in the house. I should be there in twenty minutes."

"We are in room 204, just turn right out of the elevator and its two doors on your left. Take your time and drive safely, my dear. I don't want anything to happen to you."

"You're so sweet…be there soon."

I wasn't as nervous as I was before, but I still had those feelings of anxiousness in my stomach, or was it anticipation? I know I was excited and that the butterflies were having a field day in my stomach.

I parked behind the motel and walked around to the front, again casting furtive glances around for any signs of people I knew. I walked past the reception and gave a nervous smile to the receptionist who was the same one as the last time. I'm sure he knows why we are here and what we are doing, but must see similar situations many times a day. I pressed '2' when I got into the elevator and my anticipation mounted along with my excitement. I turned right as David suggested and saw that the second door on the left was ajar. I didn't bother to knock as I opened the door. As I entered, I could not see anyone in the room, but as I advanced further, the door closed behind me and there was David, standing stark naked with a boner on.

"Oh! My God!" I said as he advanced toward me and gave me one of those awesome kisses. My hands were by my side and my right hand fell onto his erect manhood. My purse was in my left hand and I dropped it to place my arm around his neck. We kissed softly at first, but then more passionately as our tongues came into play and I rubbed my hand up and down his rock-hard cock. All feelings of anticipation and anxiousness had now been replaced with feelings of desire and wanting. We broke the embrace and I said, "That was quite a surprise reception."

"Didn't want to waste valuable time with you by undressing," he said smiling.

"Well, now you are going to have to undress me."

He smiled that infectious smile and I just melted as he cupped my breasts in his hands. He then reached for the buttons of my blouse and undid them ceremoniously by giving me a kiss, then undoing a button. After the fifth kiss and last button, he peeled the garment from my shoulders and let it fall to the floor. He sighed at my breast, held captive by the brassiere that created a bulging cleavage.

"You have exquisite breasts...let me set them free," he said as he reached around my back for the clasp, kissing the tops of each breast as he did. The garment came free and joined my blouse on the floor.

"Beautiful," he uttered as he cupped one in each hand and kissed them each in turn, sucking on the erect nipples. My breathing was now staccato as I revelled in the wonderful feelings I was now experiencing. As he continued sucking my nipples, he removed his hands and sought out the zipper on the side of my skirt, dextrously sliding it down and pulling the skirt down. I was now getting quite a collection of clothing on the floor as I stepped out of my shoes and let the skirt join the rest of the pile.

He stood up straight and looked at me.

"God! You're so gorgeous."

I just smiled at him and reached for his face and gave a delicate kiss on the lips.

"You're not so bad yourself."

He guided me over to the bed and turned me so that I was facing it with him behind. I felt his kisses on the back of my neck and shoulders as his hands reached around me for my boobs. He worked his way down my back, kissing me on the shoulder blades and then the middle of my back.

"Put your hands on the bed," he instructed me.

I obeyed and took a stance with my hands resting on the bed and my legs slightly apart as I waited in anticipation for what he was about to do. He peeled my underwear from my butt and I stepped out of them. All my clothing was now on the floor! I felt his soft mouth and gentle hands as they inched further down my back. His hands then softly caressed my ass, then down between my legs to the spot that has been yearning for him. I sighed as he touched me there and started to massage the folds of flesh. I wanted to touch him, feel him, yet felt constrained by the position I was in. All I could do was concentrate on what he was doing to me. He was kissing the cheeks of my ass as he continued to fondle my pussy. I was so wet and knew that it wouldn't be long before the waves of an orgasm overtook me. I sensed that he was now kneeling behind me as his mouth traced the lower part of my butt and found its way to my waiting pussy. I could feel fingers being inserted into my vagina as the sensation of his mouth and tongue was felt between my legs. I could feel the manipulations of my clit with his thumb as he finger-fucked me. I knew I was close and I'm sure he sensed it too. He removed his fingers and I could feel now that he had my whole pussy in his mouth…his tongue caressing my clit while alternately sucking on my labia. I felt the wave of an orgasm start and it welled up in me until it exploded and I cried out in ecstasy.

My legs felt weak as did my arms and I wanted to collapse on the bed, but I felt him stand behind me as he continued to fondle my pussy. Then I felt his cock there as he manipulated it around to moisten it with my juices, then I cried out again as he plunged it inside me and rammed against my cervix. I had to admit that I had fantasized about this position but never done it that way. It was awesome as he was able to penetrate almost to the point of hurting me, but it was a sweet rapture. I steadied myself with my arms as he pounded away at me, grunting with each thrust in tune to my sighs. The sounds of sex were music to my ears as our utterances were punctuated with the slapping of his groin on my ass. I could feel that a second orgasm was on its way and cried out again as it overtook me with surges of muscular contractions. When I was done, he stopped and pulled out. I stood up, turned around, reached for him and kissed this wonderful man with all the passion I had within me. I wanted to be joined with him again but also wanted to take him into my mouth. He guided me to the bed and laid me down, lying next to me. When he reached over to kiss me, I pushed him back to the bed and said, "My turn."

I started by kissing him on his chest and nipples, listening to his sighs of pleasure as I worked my way down. I reached for his member and started stroking it. God! I so wanted it in my mouth and had to pace myself, because I also wanted to kiss his awesome body. I was finally there and I smelled the sweet scent of him again. I enveloped the glans with my tongue and gently sucked on it, enjoying again the sounds of pleasure coming from him. I pictured the scenes from "Deep Throat" and thought I would try to swallow all of him. He wasn't huge compared to some of the studs in the movie, but big enough. I slid my mouth down his shaft until I could feel it press against the back of my throat. I tried to swallow it more but got a gag reflex, so stopped there. I could feel his excitement mounting and knew he was close. He tried to lift me from him and I said, "No, I want to do this. I want to taste you."

He smiled at me and said, "That's fine by me."

I continued sucking vigorously on the glans while jerking him off with my hand. I felt him harden as he groaned and then I sensed his cum in my mouth as he cried out. It was warm and thick and I swallowed it right away before the next salvo came. It had an odd taste, nothing like I had tasted before, but not objectionable. I remembered how Debbie had said it was an acquired taste. Each time he ejaculated into my mouth, I swallowed it and waited for the next one. This was an amazing feeling to drink the love juices of this man, a feat of which I would never have thought myself capable. As the last of the semen oozed out of his wonderful cock, I gently sucked on it and stroked it slowly. I could feel him become flaccid and I kissed the top and laid back next to him.

"You're fucking amazing," he said.

"I've never done that before and it felt awesome," I admitted.

"For something you've never done before, that was absolutely spectacular."

"Thank you."

We chatted for a while and soon he said he had to go…and so did I. I gathered my clothing from the floor and got dressed. We kissed and bade each other good bye, promising to meet again soon.

FIVE

Over the next few months, we met on average once a week and tried various positions to mix things up a little. I was fine with the different positions, but my favourite was still with me on top, cowgirl-style, because it gave me more control and I found that I could stimulate my clitoris better, while watching the looks of pleasure on his face. Although I like the 'Doggie Style' position for good penetration, it lacked the dual contact. However, for oral, I actually preferred individual stimulation of each other rather than the mutual '69' position.

It was during one of our après sex talks that he asked if I had ever been in a threesome.

"Are you kidding?" I said. "With my sexual history all I ever did was fuck. I haven't experienced so much variety in sex until I met you. How about you?"

"I have done it once…it was kinda neat, having to choreograph moves with two women."

"Why not two men?"

"I'm fine with that too. I have enjoyed a man before and although it certainly isn't my preference it's all about the whole sexual experience. I presume you've never had another woman?"

"No, but the idea somewhat intrigues me."

"Do you have another woman in mind who may want to join us? Are you OK with me touching another woman?"

"I'm OK with that seeing as it would be part of a lovemaking process. Try to fuck another woman without me though and I'll cut your balls off!"

"And I'm sure you would," he said as he smiled and kissed me. "You have no fears on that issue…you are the only woman I want."

Angela's Seduction

The next time I saw Deborah for lunch, and I mentioned that he wanted to try a threesome I was surprised by her response.

"Hey, Angie Babe. Count me in!"

I looked in awe at her, not able to believe what she said.

"Are you serious?"

"Why not? He's a good looking hunk and I wouldn't mind having you share him with me."

I was still somewhat in shock. Deborah and I had been friends since high school and I had never even considered her for a third in a ménage à trois. However, when I started to let it sink in, I had to admit that she was a very attractive woman and sometimes I did look at her with a certain amount of lust, but always discarded it as 'forbidden'.

"Look, Deborah. I must admit that when I mentioned that, I had no thoughts of you being the third person. Not that I wouldn't consider it."

"Babe," she said. "I have experienced a few women in my time and I wouldn't be honest if I said I haven't had desires on you. I just never considered it because I figured you were not into that. But with your coming out sexually with David, you've probably realized that you are a very sexual person and that sexuality is not always confined to someone of the same sex."

I thought about what she said and she was right. Since meeting David I had often logged on to porn sites and watched various movies to 'learn' what to do. Whereas the pictures of well-hung men did make me salivate somewhat, I was surprised at how the pussy pictures actually stimulated me. Now that I was not so reserved, it opened up many possibilities for sex, including sex with another woman.

"This is a lot to digest at the moment. I'm sure David will want a pic of you. Can I show him one on your Facebook page?"

"Sure, but let me look at the current one…I may want to change it."

"OK. Boy! This is some revelation. I can hardly keep up with all the changes in me over the last few months."

"But are you happy Kiddo?"

"With David? Yes, very happy. He is the balance in my life right now. Even though Peter is doing well at the AA meetings and has been on the wagon for over two months now, there is still no intimacy in our relationship. I guess there never really was."

I went back to work and thought more about having Deborah as a partner in our sexcapades. The more I thought about it the more I became agreeable to the idea. I had never really looked at Debbie from a sexual point of view before, except in the mildest 'wonder-what-it-would-be-like' scenarios. But she certainly was a beautiful woman, well-proportioned with long black hair and very generous breasts. I texted David and said:

Hi Sexy. I talked to my friend Debbie and when I said that you wanted to try a threesome, she said to count her in. I was shocked initially, but on further consideration, she would make a good partner. Next time we meet, I will show you a pic of her. Love, Angie xxx

The reply came within a few minutes:

That's awesome Baby...as long as you're OK with it. Just remember that you are the only one for me and you have my word that we will never meet in private behind your back." Love, David xoxox

I didn't answer right away as I wanted to finish some things I was doing at work. I received a text from Debbie:

Hey Angie. Found a photo you can use. See attached.

There was an attachment and I opened it. It certainly was a nice photo of her taken last year when she was on vacation in Europe, evident by the picture of the Eiffel Tower in the background. I forwarded the text to David with a note attached 'This is Deborah".

A few minutes later, I got David's reply:

Angela's Seduction

Thank you Angie for the pic. She certainly is an attractive woman and if it's OK with you, then it's fine with me.

I left it at that and went back to my work. Over the past few months I have experienced more sex than I have had in my whole life…and great sex to boot. It was amazing that I was now going to try a threesome not only with another woman, but with my best friend for twenty some years! I had to admit that my life has never been so fulfilling. I had broken out of a shell that had encapsulated me for so long, holding my feelings entrapped and my emotions enslaved by closed-mind thinking. It was a part of me that I kept secret, except for Debbie, because who in my normal life would begin to understand the transformations I have made? I was like a caterpillar that had transformed into a butterfly.

Our next planned meeting was on Tuesday and I asked David if he wanted me to invite Debbie and he said sure, so I sent a text to Debbie.

Hi Debbie. David and I are meeting Tuesday at 2:00 and we would like you to join us if you are available. David thinks you're hot…lol

Both Debbie and I had iPhones, so the messages went as an iMessage instead of a text. I could see from the screen that she was composing a reply and I waited for it.

I can make it Tuesday at 2:00. Is it at the Slumber Inn?

I replied:

Yes it is. That's great. C U there.

Wow! This was something. I was not only going to have illicit sex with my lover, but my best girlfriend is going to join in. Holy shit! What the hell am I getting myself into?

The more I thought about having Debbie join us the more excited I got. The mere fact that we were going to be intimate with each other, the more it changed the way I felt about her. Yes, we were good friends and have been for many years, but she was also a very attractive and desirable woman and since my outlook on sex in general had changed over the last few months I started to appreciate the physical side of her. As many times that I have fantasized about being with a woman, wondering what it felt like to feel someone else's tits other than your own and actually eat pussy. I was getting wet just thinking about it.

Tuesday came and I had the same nervous tension I did when I was first seeing David. The knots were back in my stomach at the thought of having sex with Deborah. How would we orchestrate it? I guess David had done it before and should be able to decide who was to do what, and with which, and to whom. David texted me the room number and I forwarded it to Debbie. I got a text back from Debbie:

Hey Babe. I don't want to be there before you, so text me when you are in the room.

Makes sense, I thought. That could be an awkward moment with David and Deborah meeting before I got there. I noticed Debbie's car was in the parking lot when I arrived as well as David's. 'The gang's all here' I mused to myself. I think the motel receptionist seemed to be expecting me as I walked into the lobby and he gave me a curt nod. 'Eat your heart out' I thought to myself.

The door was ajar as David always left it. He got up from the bed as I entered the room and walked over to greet me with that wonderful smile.

"Are you sure you're OK with this?" He asked, planting one of those awesome kisses on me.

"I'm OK. Sounds like it will be fun. I just…I just don't want you to cum inside her, OK?"

"That's fine with me Baby…it has to be right for everybody."

"I'm just going to text Debbie to come ahead. She is in the parking lot and didn't want to come up before I got here."

'OK," he said as I sent the text to her.

She replied:

Angela's Seduction

Be right up!

David and I embraced and kissed while we waited for Debbie. I could feel his hardness and my own wetness and had to slow it down until she arrived. A few minutes later there was a rap on the door and I opened it. Debbie looked gorgeous in a way I had never looked at her before and I stood aside to let her in.

"This is David," I said. "David. Deborah."

"So nice to meet you," Debbie said as she offered her hand. "Angie has told me so much about you. David took her hand and shook it, then reached over and gave her a kiss on the cheek.

"Nice to meet you too, and soon you will find out if what she said was true."

This seemed to lighten the somewhat awkward moment as we all stood there looking at each other. David stepped forward and put a hand on Debbie's and my shoulders and turned us to face each other.

"Let's see how good friends you really are," he said. With that he placed a hand behind each of our heads and eased our faces together. I wanted so much to kiss Debbie that I didn't hesitate to open myself to her. She also met my kiss with enthusiasm. I was not prepared for what I felt when our mouths met. When David and I had kissed for the first time, it was something out of this World and exceeded anything I had previously experienced. But this kiss was also spectacular, but in a different way. It was so soft and titillating and my arousal meter shot from five up to ten. For the moment, I even forgot that David was in the room until I noticed his hands on me and could feel him undressing me. I sensed also that he was doing the same to Debbie. We continued kissing and embracing and now I could feel my bare breasts against hers, which heightened my arousal even more. We were both naked now, stepping out of the clothes as David removed them without breaking contact.

"Hey," he said. "Can I join in?"

Debbie and I broke the embrace and could see that David was also naked and hard as rock. I looked at Debbie and she acknowledged what I had in mind and we each pushed him onto the bed. With Deb on one side and me on the other, we positioned ourselves around David's erect cock and I took him in my hand and stood him up. Debbie covered it with her mouth as I slowly manipulated the shaft. The groans of pleasure were emanating from him as he lay there and enjoyed the attention. I started licking one side of his cock while Debbie licked the other, and when we got to the top, we gave each other a kiss. We did this for some time until we felt an imminent climax from him and we stopped. Debbie cocked her leg over him and worked her way up to his face while I did a reverse cowgirl and pumped his dick with my pussy. I wanted to taste Debbie's pussy and eased her to lay on her back. David tried to move in position on top of her, but I encouraged him to straddle her face so she could suck his cock. I placed myself between Debbie's legs and marvelled at the wonderful sight of her pussy. She had generous labia, as had I, with neatly trimmed pubic hair. It looked so inviting, but I wanted to pace myself and not dive right in. She was sucking frantically on David's dick and I started to kiss the inside of her thighs and worked my way to the place where they met. I licked her on each side of her pussy and then placed my tongue gently on her clitoris. I'm sure the reaction I got was from me and not David as I flicked her clit with my tongue. I ran my tongue down to her vagina and tongue-fucked her with it, thinking that the next time I was here…and I had made up my mind there was definitely going to be a next time…it would just be her and me.

I sucked on her labia, rolling the flesh around between my tongue and inside cheeks. I just loved it and didn't want to stop. I could see that David had dismounted from Debbie and was now kissing her. I kept on doing what I was doing and could feel that she was going to climax, which excited me even more. Her cries were stifled by David's mouth on hers as she convulsed wildly, bucking her ass with each spasm.

David turned Debbie onto her knees and moved me below her so that I could continue eating her pussy…I guess he could sense how much I was enjoying it. He straddled both of us and inserted his cock into Debbie's pussy right above my face. I alternately licked his cock and her pussy as he proceeded to pound her with it. His balls were slapping on my chin as he buried himself deep within her. After many times hearing him cum before, I knew he was on the verge. At the precise moment he was there, I reached up and eased him out so that I could take his cum in my mouth. I opened my mouth to catch what I could, but most of it spurted over my face and I swallowed the few drops I caught in my mouth. I had got to 'acquire' the taste of his semen and loved it in my mouth, more for what it signified than for its delectableness. He dismounted and lay back on the bed. Debbie came up to me and proceeded to lick the sperm off my face and place it in my mouth with her amazing tongue and kisses. I think this is by far the wildest experience I have ever had in my life…bar none!

I felt that I had somehow neglected David during our lovemaking, so I cuddled up beside him and kissed him.

"I can taste myself," he said.

"We've all tasted you," I responded giving a furtive glance in Debbie's direction. "So, how was that?"

"I don't even have words to describe it." He said. "Having sex with two amazingly beautiful and sexual women. Wow! Is all I can say."

I reached over and kissed him and Debbie did the same. Then Debbie and I kissed.

"So!" David said. "I presume you enjoyed your first FFM experience?"

I smiled at Debbie and could see something in her eyes I had never detected before. It was a look of adoration, of wanting, of…love?

"Yes," I said. "It was very nice."

* * * * *

A week or so passed after our ménage à trois and I didn't see David nor Debbie in the meantime. I was very busy at work and had some deadlines to meet. We did text and email often, but couldn't find time to meet. I wasn't sure how to approach Debbie because of how I felt about her. Something transpired in that meeting that I wasn't sure how to handle. It seemed like a gate had been opened and I was reticent to pass through it, even though in my mind I knew that what I wanted was on the other side. I texted Debbie and invited her for lunch 'to catch up' I put it.

"Hey Babe," she said as we greeted each other in the restaurant. "I guess you've been busy, huh?"

"Yeah, really busy at work."

"How's Peter doing lately?"

"He's fine, still on the wagon. We went away last weekend to Montreal and visited some of his family there."

"And David?"

"He's great. Haven't seen each other lately because of our schedules. He's pretty busy too. Andy?"

"Andy's fine…never changes. Just goes about his merry way."

"What about the guy you were seeing?"

"That's off now. Found out he was screwing someone else so I dumped him."

"Sorry," I said.

There was a moment of silence as we seemed to run out of small talk.

"Listen Deborah, about last week. What happened there? Between us?"

"I don't know but it scared me."

"Me too. It was as though David wasn't even there. I couldn't process in my mind what I was feeling…about you."

"I know, I felt it too. As much as I enjoyed David, my memories from that meeting was of you and how good you felt. You know I didn't even get to eat your pussy."

"That's right, you didn't. But I certainly got to eat yours. It was…heavenly. And I want to do it again. Soon!"

"Me too," she said as we looked at each other with adoring eyes.

"How do I handle this with David? Should I continue to see him? I still really like him."

"Let's not make any decisions about that now until we have had a chance to be together, just you and me. See if what we were feeling the other day was real. Are you ready to accept that you may be a lesbian?"

"Never really thought about putting a label on it. But if that's what it is, then so be it. OK, so where do we go from here?"

"Can you come to my place tomorrow?" She said. "It won't raise any suspicions seeing as you are often there."

"If you think that's OK, sure."

"OK. See you at noon…I will make you lunch if you're still hungry after eating my pussy."

We laughed and I said "fine."

* * * * *

I arrived at Deborah's just before noon and rang the doorbell. She hid behind the door as she opened it and when she closed it I could see why. She was dressed in a flimsy negligée that didn't hide much of her gorgeous body. She leaned over to kiss me and we embraced. It was the same amazing kiss I remembered from a week ago. So soft and erotic…a kiss based more on love than lust.

"Just a moment," she said. "I just want to call Andy and make sure he is at the office. Go ahead to the bedroom."

I heard her speak to someone and ask that he bring home some milk. She then went to the 'fridge and dumped out most of the milk into the sink.

"Always thinking ahead," I said.

"Always," she said as she renewed the kisses.

"Let me undress," I said.

"No, let me undress you."

She dextrously undid the buttons on my silk blouse, placing kisses on the tops of my breasts as she did so. She kissed my neck as she peeled the sheer fabric from my shoulders. I pulled on the small bow in front of her negligée as she reached around and unclasped my brassiere. As I tugged on the bow strings, it came undone and I removed the lacy garment. We were both standing now with bare breasts touching while we feverishly kissed. I stepped out of my shoes and our mouths were now at the same level and we continued kissing, more passionately now with tongues thrashing. I could smell the fresh smell of soap on her, yet there was another smell that was…her. I noticed this smell often when near her but it had never turned me on the way it did now.

I let my hand fall to between her legs and felt that amazing pussy through the sheer fabric of her panties, remembering the magical feeling of it in my mouth last week. I lifted my hand slightly and slid it down inside the underwear and felt the pubic hair, then the folds of flesh a little lower down. As I inserted my fingers in the folds, I could feel her wetness as I parted the labia and fondled her clit. We were still kissing, but her breathing had changed into a staccato pattern as she struggled to breathe through her nose. She reached for the zipper of my skirt and slipped it down, at the same time easing it over my ass and letting it fall to the floor. Her hand was now on my pussy as she manipulated it through my panties.

She pushed me towards the bed and I fell back onto it. She glanced at my face and smiled, then spread my legs slightly and lifted them up and kissed my toes, then my feet, right down to my thighs, kissing one leg and then the other. I was in a dream as she neared the treasured spot. It was only a few months ago that David was in this position and, at the time, it was rapturous. This time though it was more…magical, more…sensuous, more…loving. I could feel her licking the inside of my groin either side of my pussy, then I could feel her mouth on me, sucking my labia through the gossamer fabric of my underwear. She reached for the waistband of my panties and slipped them over my butt and off my legs.

"My God!" She said. "It is the most beautiful thing I have ever seen."

With that she dove into me and I could feel her mouth and tongue perform wonders on that most cherished of spots. I cried out in ecstasy at her expert manipulations and I could feel the beginnings of an orgasm as she continued to work her magic on me. I felt the waves of pleasure start to wash over me as she reached up and cupped a breast in each hand, tweaking the nipples as she did so. I could feel her slow down her movements on me as I'm sure she could sense my pending climax.

"Yes! Babe, yes!" she cried out just as I was about to explode. I could feel her mouth return to my pussy as the first wave hit me. The convulsion caused me to raise my butt as I cried out in sheer pleasure…then the second wave hit and I convulsed again. Debbie's mouth was fixed in place as her head went up and down with each convulsions, her hands firmly clamped on my breasts. As the waves subsided, I felt that all my energy had been drained and I lay there spent. Debbie was still slowly caressing my pussy with her tongue, but it seemed to be overly sensitive now and I pushed her head away.

She crawled up my body and lay on top of me, seeking out my lips with hers. I wrapped my arms around her and kissed her passionately.

"That was absolutely amazing," I said. "The best orgasm I have had by far."

"Wow!" She said. "That's quite a compliment. If it was anything like the one you gave me last week, I know what you mean."

"Give me a chance to catch my breath a bit and I'll give you another one." I promised.

She was still on top of me, gently kissing me on my face and lips. They were such loving kisses, tender and soft and full of adoration, almost idolization.

I got my second wind and rolled her off of me. I started by kissing her lovely breasts and sucking on her plump nipples, then worked my way down to her navel, gently fondling her with my hands and the tips of my fingers. The reaction from her was intoxicating and I felt so proud to be the instrument of her pleasure. I placed kisses on her groin area and let her trimmed pubic hair tickle my nose. As I approached my raison d'être, I could smell the sweet scent of her...that scent that so aroused me a week ago. I just couldn't wait to feel the wonderful feeling of her pussy again.

I was there! So thrilling, so inebriating. All my senses were being stimulated...the sound of her sighs, the sight and smell of her pussy, the taste of her juices and the feeling of my tongue on her. I slowly rolled my tongue on her clitoris...first side to side and then up and down and reveled in the response it elicited. I sucked the abundant labia into my mouth as I did last week and rolled it around with my tongue. I was in heaven, in nirvana...no other place I would rather be than here. Her sighs became more pronounced and I knew she was almost there. Her pelvis was now gyrating as the waves of pleasure overtook her. She cried out, "Oh! Yes! Yes!" As the first wave hit I held on tightly with my arms around her legs and hands clasped on her abdomen. With each successive pulse she arched her pussy and a corresponding gasp was emitted from her.

It was over. She lay there as I had done a few minutes ago, totally spent and sated. I placed gentle kisses on her clit and labia and then moved up beside her. I kissed her gently and she returned it in kind. We softly kissed for a while, then she said: "Promise you will never stop doing that to me?"

I smiled and said, "I promise."

I know this sounds crazy," she said. "But I think I am madly in love with you."

"I know, I feel the same way too."

Angela's Seduction

"This is so weird," she said.

"I'm still trying to process it all too. A month or so ago I was in a sexless marriage, then I broke out of my shell and had some amazing sex with David, and now I am in love with my best friend."

"It almost seems like we've wasted a lot of years doing other things when we should have been together."

"True," I said. "But there are many things I don't regret. Having two wonderful children for one. I'm not sure also that I would have been ready for this years ago."

"I agree that not all my life has been bad…I have had some great times with Andy and as you say, did enjoy the children. I guess we can be happy that we have found each other now."

Debbie rolled over on top of me and started kissing me again. Soft and playful kisses with the occasional tongue play. As she did this, she pressed her pubis into me and moved her pelvis so that I could feel her pubic hair on mine. I could feel her breasts and nipples on mine as she gyrated herself on top of me. It began to excite me again and the kissing became more passionate. I parted my legs slightly and she moved herself so that her pussy was rubbing on my leg. I could feel the wetness on my skin as she continued to manipulate herself on my leg. I looked into her face between kisses and was enraptured with the look of total pleasure there. After a while, I heard her breathing change and I could swear she was going to orgasm again. As she pressed herself harder into me, her sighs became grunts and then she convulsed.

"Arhh...Arhh...Arhhhh!" she cried as she orgasmed again.

"Did you just climax again on top of me?"

"Sure did," she said with a smug look on her face. "What can I say Babe? You turn me on so much."

* * * * *

69

I began to struggle with my feelings for Debbie, for David…for Peter. I was in somewhat of a quandary as to how to proceed. I really liked David and we had great sex together, but sex with Debbie was so much more meaningful. Then there was Peter, with whom I was having no sex, but there was still a sense of commitment…of responsibility. Then there were the children to consider and our network of friends. Same-sex relationships, while more accepted today, are still not understood by the many traditionalists, especially those following religious teachings. We, as a society, still feel that everyone should be like us and, as a result, tend to associate primarily with people of similar likes and dislikes. This is especially true of religious and political leanings. We form clubs and societies so that like-minded people can enjoy that which we share. Being gay will put you on the outside of virtually all of those associations and groups. I just wasn't prepared to 'come out of the closet' and face up to society's rejection, especially that by my family and friends.

I felt it was only the right thing to do to send David a message and explain that it was over…I now felt that I would be cheating on Debbie if I were to continue seeing him. I didn't want to tell him the real reason for ending it, so made an excuse that Peter was trying so hard to make things work and that I wanted to make it work too. He responded that he was naturally disappointed but in his true gentleman fashion, wished me all the best.

I then met with Debbie to discuss…'us'.

"Hey Babe", said Deb as we met for lunch at the regular restaurant, reaching over and giving me a peck on the cheek, which I returned. I wanted to plant one right on her lips and thrust my tongue down her throat, but refrained under the circumstances.

"So," I said as we sat. "What do we do?"

"About what?"

Angela's Seduction

"About us. How do we handle this? Bye the way, I sent David a message saying it was over between us…said I was trying to work things out with Peter." That elicited a smile from Debbie.

"I'm not about to tell all and bring our relationship out into the open," I said. "As much as I want to. I don't want my family and friends, and my work mates, know that I am having a same-sex relationship."

"I understand Babe. I don't want that either. It's a little easier to have an 'affair' with someone of the same sex because people generally see nothing wrong in two men or two women seeing each other behind closed doors. If we were caught together at your place or mine, we could easily pass it off as a normal meeting between two friends."

"Unless we were caught in bed doing a 69," I joked.

"That would be a little more difficult to explain."

"So, we continue seeing each other during the day at your place or mine and exercise caution," I said.

"Sure. Speaking of which, I have this great idea for dessert…"

"My place?" I said, smiling at her.

"See you there in 15," she said with a grin.

We continued seeing each other for the next few months, but it wasn't as easy as we had initially envisioned. One time we had to scramble when I heard Peter's truck drive up. Fortunately, we had just got started and weren't completely naked, but any make-up was a mess. We always had a story ready should such an occasion happen, and Peter accepted that Debbie was there helping me with colours for the bedroom. Also, while we were her place, the next door neighbour knocked on the back door and interrupted us. I was also beginning to miss David and the feel of a man inside me, so I guess I was bi and not gay. Peter was also much more attentive lately and I felt guilty because he was genuinely trying to make things better. All these things tended to confuse me as to what I really should be doing and I was feeling stressed to a point where I needed some help.

So I went to a counsellor.

I explained the whole story to her and she made notes as I spoke. When I had finished, she leaned back in her chair and paused for thought.

"I am not able to tell you what you should do," she said. "Only you can make that decision. However, I can guide you in what you need to consider in making that decision. It will not be an easy decision and will probably be the hardest one you will ever have to make."

I sat there and considered what she had said. I was kind of hoping she would just give me the answer of what I should do, but I guess that wasn't how it was going to happen.

Quite frankly, the counsellor didn't really tell me anything I didn't already know. She outlined my obligation to Peter and inserted the 'for better or for worse' quote. Then she explained the difficulties with a same-sex relationship and how that would be an issue with family and friends. Basically, she said I had two alternatives…give up Debbie and work on my marriage or leave Peter and make a life with Debbie.

I sat there for a while pondering the two alternatives. Of course, this was nothing new. I realized long ago that these were my only options. I just didn't want to accept them.

"Go away and think long and hard about this, as it will affect your life going forward. Give me a call if you want to chat more."

"OK," I said and left her office.

I did think long and hard about what she said and eventually, and reluctantly, made my decision. I knew I had to make a better effort with Peter to make things work, which meant having to give up Debbie. The very thought of doing that brought tears to my eyes. Before I changed my mind, I called Debbie and arranged lunch.

"Why the long face?" Debbie said as she sat down opposite me.

"I went to see a counsellor," I said…and then I burst into tears.

"Babe," she said and got up to comfort me. "What is it?"

I composed myself and said, "I'm OK."

Debbie went back to her chair, a look of concern on her face.

"I can't go on like this," I said sobbing. I casually looked around the restaurant to make sure I wasn't making a spectacle of myself. It was late in the day and there were very few people there. "I love you Debbie but I can't continue with the deceit and lies."

"I know Babe," she said. "I'm having problems too. I love you too…I think I always have, but wasn't sure how you felt about me. Now I know the feelings are mutual, it is harder than ever to resist you."

I looked up and smiled. I had a resolve going in to this meeting, but now she was in front of me I wasn't sure that I was going to be able to go through with it. The thought of never seeing her again, sexually, caused knots the size of melons in my stomach. I reached over to clasp her hands and squeezed them. Just the touch of her skin made me tingle and send signals to my pussy. God! I wanted her…now more than ever. As I looked into her eyes, I knew I would not be able to give her up.

"Before coming here, I had decided to try and make things work with Peter," I said. "But now I am here with you, I realize how much I love you…how important you are to me. I don't know why I ever thought I could give you up." The crying started again and Debbie came over again to comfort me. She put her arms around my shoulders and rested her head on mine.

"Hey Babe. It's OK. I know how you feel…I thought about it myself and came to the same realization that I could never give you up because I love you so much." She kissed me on the back of the head. I could smell her perfume, made unique by her own scent. I felt the wetness between my legs and knew that just being close to her aroused me.

I got up from my chair, tears streaming from my eyes, turned around and hugged her. I held her for a long time and could feel her tears on my cheek. Finally, we broke the embrace and I looked at her.

"Does my mascara look as bad as yours," I laughed.

"I'm afraid so," she said.

"I need to see you, make love to you, now!"

"I can assure you that the feeling is mutual. Let's get a room so we won't be bothered with any interruptions."

"Sounds like a great idea," I said. "Slumber Inn?"

"See you there."

We made love tenderly, each exploring each other's bodies. I went first, slowly undressing her and kissing each part of the skin that became exposed. I lingered on her nipples with soft bites, plucking them with my lips and swirling my tongue around them. I slowly kissed my way down her stomach until I got to her pussy. I didn't know that I could feel so much adoration for anything as I did for this part of Debbie. I just loved everything about being between her legs…the smell, the taste, the feel of her wetness, the sounds she made. I knew then and there that I had made the right decision not to give her up…this was now what I lived for, what I felt I was destined to do. Everything else would have to fall in place and I knew it would…as long as I had Debbie there with me. After Debbie had climaxed, she started on me and I lay back in a dreamlike trance as she expertly manipulated all my sensitive parts with her mouth, tongue and fingers. It wasn't long before I, too, exploded in a violent orgasm.

I sat down and itemized the things I had to do in order to ease into my new life. I would call Brian and Beth and explain that I was planning to leave their father…hopefully they would understand. I dreaded the conversation I was planning to have with Peter. Before I did so, I booked a room at one of the local hotels as I did not want to stay in the house after I told him I was leaving. I had already scoped out some furnished apartments to rent until I could find a place on my own. My lawyer was also drafting the separation agreement. It was time to pull the plug.

Thank you for reading my novella…I hope you enjoyed it.

I was very excited about writing my full-length novel, "Bosnian Affair" and hope that you will enjoy reading it.

BOSNIAN AFFAIR

Bosnian Affair is a thriller that blends action and suspense with erotic and romantic sequences.

Brad, a successful architect, succumbs to the alluring and beautiful interior designer, Sophia and embarks on an affair. However, things take a nasty turn when he visits her apartment and finds that she has been murdered. The book, through flashbacks, provides graphic details of their torrid affair and Brad's struggle to balance his home life and keep the affair secret. Present-day storyline outlines Brad's efforts to find her killer and seek restitution for her. During his investigation, Brad reveals a startling discovery involving a Bosnian war criminal sought after by the International Criminal Tribunal for the former Yugoslavia (ICTY) entrenched in a high-ranking position within Canada. Brad's efforts to hunt down her killer takes him to Sarajevo and Buenos Aires where he must rely on his sniper skills to eradicate him and find closure.

You can download Bosnian Affair from your favourite e-book retailer.

If you would like to be notified when new books are released, please e-mail me at authorchrisfox@gmail.com. Please also visit my Website authorchrisfox.com for updates on new releases.